Daniel Fleming

Daniel Fleming
Fifth in the
Settling The West Series

Copyright © 2018 by David Dodge
ISBN 978-1890548193
Masair Publications

Published in the United States of
America
Cover Design
By the Author

Note from the Author

The books I write are about regular people who moved into the West in order to make a home. They are the stories of those people and their struggles. They are not typical shoot-'em-up westerns, even though that was required occasionally because of the nature of man. I try to make stories that can be shared by the whole family, without foul language or overly-suggestive scenes. Occasionally a character will slip, but hopefully not so that it can't be enjoyed by the whole family.

I hope you enjoy Daniel Fleming; and if you do, there are four other books you might enjoy: **The Forbes Family, Lance Burkholt, Commodore Kelley, and Dutch Weaver**, all available on Amazon. To order from Amazon enter: David Dodge's and the title you select. It should come right up. Thank you for reading this book.

CHAPTER 1

The sky was dull and overcast, as Daniel Fleming reluctantly poked his head out of his sugan to find that a late spring snow had fallen during the night.

Having positioned his camp under the heavily needled spruce trees beside the Pecos River in New Mexico; it was spared a heavy layer of snow.

He shook out his boots, slipped on his clothes and began making a fire with the wood he had gathered the night before. Knowing that grass would be wet from the snow, he quickly went to work with his knife to get shavings that would be cut deep enough to be dry; and then he placed some of the driest grass he could find on top. When he had the fire going and coffee water set, he walked to the horses picketed close to the river. His dog, Corky, was only a step or two behind him. When they were close to the horses, the dog found a dry spot close to the trunk of a tree and curled up there to watch.

Daniel began rubbing them down to restore more circulation into them. "Got a little cool last night didn't it, Latigo?" The horse he was rubbing was the horse he rode. Latigo

3

turned his head around and bumped Daniel in the back with his nose.

When he had finished all the horses, he moved back to the fire where his coffee water was boiling, so he dropped a handful of coffee into the blackened pot.

"Son," he heard a groan. "Go wake up Mrs. Fleming."

"Ah . . . okay, Poppa," he replied. Then as he crawled out of his bed he exclaimed, "Hey! It snowed last night, Corky!" The little dog crawled back into the bed.

Daniel witnessed the action of the boy and the dog. "It did snow last night, but not enough to give us trouble. The trail looks clear so we shouldn't have any deadfalls."

"Mom! . . . Mom! It snowed last night!"

"I heard you talking about it, son."

"Pop said it's time to get up. Coffee's ready."

"And I'm ready for it. I got cold last night!" she informed them.

"Tonight you can bunk in with me," said Daniel.

She looked at him, and then said, "I'd rather slide in with Adam; he gives off more heat, and doesn't turn all night like you do."

"Very well, if you change your mind the offer is still open. Why don't you get the bacon and the fish Adam caught last night going on the fire; I'll start getting the equipment on the packhorses ready so we can leave right after breakfast."

"As soon as I get dressed and you get the skillet for me," she responded.

Adam was working in the background and hollered, "Look ya'll, I built a snowman!"

His dad looked at him and commented, "Kinda small isn't he?"

"Yeah . . . couldn't scrape up much snow. It's melting kinda fast."

Jennifer, his mother, said, 'It's cute anyway, even if it won't last long."

Daniel Fleming is the son of the late Hamish and Ainslie Fleming, immigrants from Cruden Bay near Aberdeen, Scotland. Since coming to the States, he had traveled across the nation working as a cowhand. While working in Oklahoma for a sheriff's office, he had met and eventually married Jennifer Little Bird.

Daniel was tall, six three, with dark complexion and thick auburn hair, brown eyes and a smile to light up the morning.

Jennifer Fleming, wife of Daniel Fleming and mother of Adam Fleming, had just turned twenty eight last month. She was a tall, straight-standing beauty with black hair and dark eyes. She was part Cherokee Indian and looked it. Her slightly tan complexion was as smooth as silk. Because of her mixed race, she was brought up and educated in the home of the Indian agent close to the Three Rivers Nation near Muskogee, Oklahoma. Her mother was Cherokee and her father was a French trapper who had drifted west from trapping along the Mississippi River and had moved on.

Their son, Adam, was eight years old, large for his age, and proficient at ranch work.

Daniel had been working for a ranch in Montana, and was moving his family to North Texas to the headquarters of the XIT Ranch, where he was to take on one of their farms.

"Have you got everything together?"

"Yep, we have, Poppa. Everything is packed and we're ready."

"Well, mount up and let's move on; we've a ways to go." Mounting, he said, "We'll load up on supplies at Pecos as we go through."

As they rode along the river they were closed in on both sides by the large rocks and walls that over the millennia had been cut by the Pecos River.

"It will take a while to get to Pecos, so we'll stop about midday to fix a bit of lunch. Adam, do you think you could catch a couple of trout pretty quick so we can have them with lunch?" asked Daniel.

"Yes, sir, they bite on that old cheese pretty good. I make little balls to put on the hook. We don't have a lot left, but we have enough I can catch us lunch."

"All right, I'll get you more cheese at Pecos. We'll travel along the river for quite some time. You can catch 'em and I'll clean 'em. Remind me to get some more cheese when we get supplies. We'll stop before long. Are you doing all right Mrs. Fleming?"

"Doing fine, Mr. Fleming I am ready to stop just anytime, though."

"Okay, then. I see a widening area in the trail coming up; we'll stop there."

"Wish we could live along here, Daniel; it's really beautiful," observed Jennifer.

"It is beautiful country, but here in the Sangre De Christo Mountains the snow covers this area a lot of the winter."

Grimacing, she said, "Maybe I *don't* want to live here."

With a big smile on his face, Adam spoke up. "I know I would. I could make big snowmen, and I could make a sled so Corky could pull me."

"*Then* what would you do? Sit by the fire all day?" mused Daniel.

"I guess I could play in the snow with Corky."

"Say, where is that dog anyway?"

"He was chasing something a while ago," said Adam.

Daniel looked the open area over, and decided it would make a good place to stop.

"We have easy access to the river here and Adam can fish while I get a fire started for some coffee. Wait a minute, Mrs. Fleming, and I'll help you down."

"You go ahead and find some wood. I can get down okay," she responded.

The area he had chosen was wide enough to spread a tarp from one of the sugans for them to sit on. Adam managed to catch fish for their lunch, and as promised, Daniel cleaned them and readied them for the skillet.

"What's Corky barking at?" asked Daniel.

Adam laughed. "There's a squirrel on the branch of that tree barking at him . . . he's just barking back."

When they broke this camp, they got supplies at Pecos. It wasn't long before they exited the wilderness and moved out on the plains-type terrain. They would follow the Pecos River as far as Fort Sumner and then move east to the ranch where they were to work. Daniel would be working on one of the XIT Ranch's farms, and she would cook for those who worked on the farm. The XIT, located in the Texas panhandle, stretched across three million acres. It was established when Texas offered the land to the Farwell brothers of Chicago to build the capitol of Texas.

Jennifer rode up close to Daniel. "Daniel, I've heard of Fort Sumner. They made the Indians walk for hundreds of miles and tried to make farmers out of them, but most of them died. I don't want to go there."

"You won't have to, dear; they closed the fort and the Indian project a long time ago, but we can still get supplies in the town of Fort Sumner."

As they traveled on toward Fort Sumner, Daniel noticed the railroad coming up from the south, and then turning toward the town.

"When we get into town to buy our supplies, I think I'll check on the railroad."

"Check what?" Jennifer asked.

"About the railroad and how we might take it east. The river goes south from here and if we go east to the ranch we won't have a lot of water like we've had traveling along the Pecos. Aboard the train we won't have to worry about water.

"I didn't know they had a railroad this far south, yet."

"It's brand new. It's the Atchison, Topeka and Santa Fe. It runs all the way to Lubbock.

"Then, why don't I get the supplies and you check on that?"

"You sure you don't mind?"

"Adam and I will be all right," she responded.

"Okay then I'll see you two as soon as I find out something."

Daniel headed to the depot, stepped up on the slanted end of the loading dock, then walked up to the open door.

He looked in but didn't see a ticket window.

A man in the back hollered out to him, "Ticket office is outside and around the corner."

"Thanks," said Daniel as he went out the door.

When he found the ticket window, he approached it and knocked on the window. After a moment a crusty old timer came to the window. He had a thick mustache turned a little brown from his chewing tobacco.

"Need a little help?" he asked.

Daniel stifled a laugh when he saw the old man vigorously chewing his cud of tobacco. "Yes sir. I'd like to find out about some tickets east."

The old man paused his chewing and asked, "Just fer yerself?"

"No, sir, me, my wife, son, and four horses. Oh, and my dog," answered Daniel.

"Well, sir, you'll have to wait 'till tomorrow. Train with that much room comes about eleven thirty. Where ye headed?"

"North Texas. Lookin' at your chart, we probably need to ride as far as Lubbock. We'll have to ride the horses north from there," said Daniel.

"You plan to take yore own horse feed?"

"What's the price of that?"

"Well, less see . . . it's five dollars if we furnish the hay fer the horses, three dollars if you furnish yore own."

"That's pretty reasonable. I can take along a bit of grain because they won't need much since they won't be workin. How much then for my wife and boy?"

"How old is the boy?"

"He's eight."

"That's good. He won't cost you nuthin'. Let's see ... two to Lubbock, Texas . . . that'll cost ya ...I recon you'll want to eat?"

"Yes, we will; some, anyway."

"Rounded off, it comes to four dollars and fifty three cents."

"Okay, let's do it. Tomorrow . . . eleven thirty, right?"

"Shore 'nuff. I'll see you then."

Daniel proceeded to the general store where he left Jennifer and Adam, stepped up on the loading dock and walked in.

Jennifer looked toward the door and saw Daniel approaching. "Just in time! I need a he-man to carry these supplies, and put them on the pack horse!"

"That's what I'm here for."

"You're *so* accommodating, dear."

"I try to be. We are all set to take the train to Lubbock. Unfortunately we have to ride from there to our new home, but it won't be far. The ranch starts north of Lubbock."

"That will be a blessing. I get a little sore on the long distances."

"If you like, we can buy a buckboard in Lubbock. We can always use it later."

"That sounds tempting, but I'll think about that later. Why don't you find us a place to stay tonight?"

"I'll do just that, and find a place to eat, too. I see Adam is eying the candy; did you get any for him?"

"I got his favorite… peppermint."

Daniel, with a big smile confessed, "Just happens to be my favorite, too."

CHAPTER 2

Next morning, the Fleming family stood together on the railroad platform as the big black engine slowly pulled into the station. Steam engulfed them as it pulled to a stop.

Adam gleefully spoke loud over the noise made by the big steam engine. "I've never been this close to a train before. It's big!"

Jennifer leaned over toward him and agreed. "Yes, it is big, and we're going to ride on it for a while."

"Oh boy, that'll be fun. When can we get on?"

"As soon as that man wearing the black cap, the one that just stepped off the train, yells, 'All Aboard'."

"What does that mean, mom?"

"It means everyone that's riding the train is to get on board."

"On board?" he questioned.

"Yes it means to get on the train," she explained.

"I'm ready now!" Adam shouted.

"Still, it'll be a little while yet. He gives everyone time to get a ticket."

"Do we have a ticket?" he asked.

"Yes; your Dad has them."

Daniel approached Jennifer and Adam. "I got all the horses and Corky loaded. The man said he would take good care of them. I got a few snacks from our pack, but he said they feed so good we may not need them."

Jennifer smiled. "Adam will, no matter how good the food is."

"Yes, I know. That's why I brought the snacks."

The steam gushed from the side of the engine and a loud voice shouted, "All Aboard!"

The Fleming family stepped up into the passenger coach, moved inside, and took a seat near the door.

"Can I sit by the window, mother?"

"*May* I sit by the window?"

"But, Mom I want to sit by the window."

"I meant for you to ask with *may I*, not *can I*."

"Oh, I see," he answered. "Well, may I?"

"Yes, you may."

Smiling, Daniel said, "Now that that's settled, scoot in there before I sit by the window."

The train started to roll out of the station. "We're on our way!" exclaimed Adam. "Hey, where's Corky?"

"He had to ride in the baggage car," Daniel responded.

"Well, he'll be okay won't he?"

"He'll be fine; don't worry."

The rocking of the coach and the clicking of the wheels on the end of each rail, made for easy dozing for Daniel, but Adam took in every scene passing the train window.

"Look, Mom! That antelope is running as fast as the train is moving!"

"He's scared and trying to get away," explained Jennifer.

"I wish I could run that fast."

It wasn't long before Adam and Jennifer were asleep. Daniel's attention was drawn to the rapidly passing scenes outside the window, but it was hard for him to keep his eyes open.

The afternoon sun was in a position to cast the shadow of the coach where Daniel could see it out the opposite window. After a few minutes he saw the shadow of a man walking on top of the coach.

He murmured half out loud, "That's strange. Why would someone be walking on the top of the coach?"

He turned and looked out his side of the coach and saw a rider running at a slightly faster speed than the train was going; he was leading four saddled horses.

"That could only be a robbery in progress," he mumbled.

He roused Jennifer from her sleep. "Jen, wake up. Take this pistol; we may be having a robbery. I don't know what this train might be carrying, but if it's not much, they may rob the passengers. Keep the gun out of sight until you have to use it. I'm goin to check this out."

"Daniel, be careful." He heard her say as he walked away, "A lawman too long."

Daniel had served in the sheriff's office in Oklahoma a long time before he had married Jennifer.

He exited the coach slowly, so as to not cause any angst among the other passengers. The coach was tied directly to the baggage car. Daniel stood on the platform between the cars when he heard a shot from inside the baggage car. He tried to look around the side of the coach, when a shot splintered wood just above his head.

Daniel turned to see the man leading the horses getting ready for another shot. Daniel's gun slid into his hand and he shot the man before he could take another shot. The horses he was leading split and went in all directions.

Another shot, narrowly missing Daniel, came from a man half hanging out the door of the express car. Daniel just waited to see if the man would take a second shot. There wasn't long to wait; the man leaned out the door and when he did, Daniel shot him and he fell from the train.

Daniel thought: *the man had three extra horses . . . that means two more are in the express car.*

The men inside must have figured it wasn't a good idea to hang out the door since one that did was shot; so Daniel climbed to the top of the express car and moved to the spot over the open doorway.

Daniel decided to just ride on the top of the express car to the next town that had a sheriff. They couldn't escape because the only way out was through the big door and he was watching for them.

The next town would be Clovis, New Mexico, and then after that Farwell, Texas. One or the other should have a sheriff and a jail.

One of the men stuck his head out as if to jump, so Daniel placed a shot so near him that he backed into the car.

He yelled to them, "I'm riddin' up here 'till we get to a jail. If the express guard is shot I just may shoot all of you anyway."

He could hear one of them yell back, "He ain't been shot, but he may be if you don't let us go!"

"You might get real acquainted with him and take good care of him, because if anything happens to him, you won't come out of this alive."

Daniel rode that way until the train pulled into Clovis.

As the train slowly rolled into the station, the station master walked out from the station, Daniel called out to him, "Don't go into the express car; go get the sheriff."

He looked questioningly at Daniel on top of the car. "What's going on?"

"Don't worry about it; just get the sheriff . . . **Now!**"

"Okay, okay; I'm going."

Passengers began to drift out of the passenger car, and Daniel told them, "We won't be long, so go back in and have a seat. The sheriff is comin' and when he takes the prisoners, we will be on our way."

Soon Sheriff Warren Pickens came and stepped up on the loading dock.

"Howdy, Sheriff, I'm Daniel Fleming. You'll find a couple of men in that car who wanted to take somethin' that didn't belong to them. I promised them if the guard was hurt they would be in trouble. I sure would appreciate you takin' care of them so's I can get down off this car. It just isn't too comfortable, and I've been up here for an hour or so."

Sheriff Pickens looked up at Daniel and said, "Young man, you may not know it, but you just saved a shipment worth a hundred and fifty thousand dollars headed to Lubbock. Sheriffs up and down the line have been alerted. I suppose someone talked about it or was part of this outfit. I thank you and I'll take care of these fellers so come on down. The train will be headed to Lubbock as soon as I check everything out." Then he shouted, "You men in the baggage car throw out your guns. My deputy will be here in a minute to ride along with the guard as far as Lubbock."

"Thank you Sheriff . . . Pickens was it?"

"Yes, that's right."

"I'm sure glad you were here. I'm not sure I could have made it to Lubbock. It's not easy on the backside hanging over the edge makin' sure they didn't jump off."

"There are at least two men along the track that thought they could hit me on this movin' train. They'll be there when you send someone to look for them."

Daniel climbed down the ladder, shook hands with Sheriff Pickens, and went into the passenger car to where Jennifer and Adam sat.

When he sat down, Jennifer moved close, took hold of his arm and said, "You worked with the Oklahoma Sheriff's Department too long. Did everything work out?"

"Yes. Thank goodness there was a sheriff here, because I don't think my backside would have lasted much farther."

"Where were you?"

"Sittin' on top of a boxcar!"

"What were you doing sitting on a boxcar?"

"Making sure some would-be thieves didn't get off the train."

"What were they after?" she asked.

"About a hundred and fifty thousand dollars."

"That's a lot of money; someone will be grateful."

"I suppose so, but I was really afraid they might steal our horses."

She pushed him and said, "Oh, you . . . "

He leaned over and kissed her.

CHAPTER 3

That evening a tall, nice-looking man in a white coat sauntered through the coach striking a small triangle while announcing dinner was being served in the dining car.

Passengers began to move toward the back of the car and into the next car.

Tables with white cloths lined both sides of the car. Menus were on the table, as were flat ware and water glasses.

The waiter poured water in glasses as he moved through the coach. When Adam's glass was filled, he was mesmerized by the water shaking back and forth without the glass turning over.

"Mom . . . look! Little rings go from the middle of the glass to the outside, one right after the other!"

"Yes, Adam, and if you will listen you will hear a click of the wheels each time a circle is started in the glass."

"The wheels are what cause the water to move?" he asked.

Daniel smiled and said, "Yes, the wheels hitting the crack between where the rails are joined together causes the car to move up and down a small amount, and that is transferred up into the body of this car. Be real still and you can feel it too."

". . . I feel it, Pop."

Daniel smiled and asked, "Now do you understand why the rings are formed in the glass?"

"Yes sir, I understand *how* they are formed, but I don't know *why*."

"Let's just say it's to entertain you . . . here comes our food."

Jennifer's eyes got larger. "Oh, Daniel, this looks so good, and I didn't have to fix it!"

"And I'll bet it's as good as it looks," he agreed.

When the train pulled into the station in Lubbock, the passengers exited the train and stood on the station platform which was filled with town's people. A man in a grey suit stepped closer to the passengers who gathered on the platform. He peered over his gold rim glasses as he loudly announced, "I'm looking for a Daniel Fleming."

Daniel walked toward the man. "I'm Daniel Fleming, at your service."

"I'm Terrance Bridges, and I received a wire from Sheriff Pickens that explained what you did to save the shipment. Well, our board, at the hospital feels that your service deserves a reward. Had it not been for you, we would not be able to build our planned expansion to serve more of the people who live in the surrounding area. I am pleased to present you this check for five hundred dollars and a small plaque as a token of our appreciation."

"I don't know what to say or how to thank you, sir. I was just doing what seemed to me the right thing to do."

"I surmise, sir, that at some time you have been in the employ of a law office."

"You would surmise right. Please thank your board members. Now my family and I can afford a much-needed buckboard to ride to our destination."

"Well, sir, I would be perfectly pleased if you took possession of mine. I'll get my things out of it. You may never know how indebted to you we are. We have worked for years to come up with the money for this expansion."

"I don't want to take your ride, sir."

"No problem! We have several we use at the hospital to obtain the supplies we need. Often it takes a buckboard to obtain the heavy supplies, so we have them handy."

Daniel looked at the check and then at Mister Bridges. "Once again, I don't know what to say."

Jennifer stepped closer to the two men and said, "Sir, our family thanks you and your hospital, and we hope the expansion goes well."

By-standers applauded loudly.

Daniel unloaded the horses from the train and placed the saddles, packs, and Corky in the buckboard, then harnessed his own horse to Mister Bridges' buckboard. Terrance Bridges removed his property, and then helped

Jenifer onto the seat. Daniel lifted Adam and placed him on the seat beside her and Corky jumped into Jennifer's lap.

"Can I drive?"

Jennifer frowned and said, "Remember Adam. It's "may I" drive?

"I'm sorry, Mom. It's hard to remember sometime."

Daniel took the reins from Adam and said, "I'll show you how after we get out of town so there won't be anything to run into."

"Okay, I'll watch you."

"Good! Suppose we find a place to stay," suggested Daniel.

"I'm ready to find a place to eat," said Jennifer."

"Me, too," agreed Adam.

Daniel popped the reins and said, "Suits me."

Daniel pulled up in front of the only hotel in town, tied the horse to the hitching post, dropped the anchor, and they went inside.

Daniel headed toward the check in desk. "Good day, sir. Are they still serving meals?"

The clerk at the desk had looked up when he saw them come in and greeted them. When he saw Jennifer and Daniel, he said, "Mister, if I was you I'd go to the boarding house a couple of doors down."

"Why is that?"

He moved close to Daniel and said, A little ranch called the BZ started up a while back and hired in a few questionable characters who have been stirring up trouble ever since. Especially hard on the Indians around these parts, if you know what I mean. When I noticed your lady . . .

Daniel interrupted. "She's my wife!"

"Yes, sir, I just thought you might avoid trouble by going elsewhere. They're in there now, and I think they came directly from the saloon."

"I see . . . probably better not to push our luck. I'm not in the mood to shoot anybody else today." So they left.

At the boarding house, Daniel tied the horse and told Corky to stay in the buckboard.

They were serving family style, so Jennifer led the family in and a lady showed them three seats at one of the large tables. She said, "Help yourself. My name is Grace Sewell. We're glad to have you."

Adams eyes got big when he saw the cherry pie at the end of the table. "Mom, look! My favorite, cherry pie!"

"No pie until you eat, Adam".

"Aw, Mom," he said sadly.

"Just look at what they have: you like fried chicken and smashed potatoes, as you call them. Eat, and then you can have cherry pie.

The server brought coffee for Daniel and Jennifer, and milk for Adam.

After the meal, Daniel asked if there were rooms to rent just for overnight. The server said there were a few rooms which rented over night, but most were leased to people who stayed for longer periods. "If you will knock on the door of number three, Elizabeth will fix you up."

"Thank you, we enjoyed the meal very much," said Jennifer.

"I'll let Georgia know you enjoyed her cooking," she responded with a warm smile.

Daniel knocked on number three, and when the door opened he said, "Howdy, Miss Elizabeth. My family and I would like to rent a room for tonight."

"Oh, you're the feller who saved our hospital. The one they were honoring today!" she said excitedly.

"I would be the one."

"Why, sure we have a room for you. I'll make it easy for you. The one next door, number two, that away you won't have to carry your stuff so far. At least not up those stairs."

"I'm much obliged to you, ma'am."

One of John Holton's men had seen them come in and ran to tell him.

"Boss, that guy the town honored that beat us out of the money just checked in at the boardin' house. Just for tonight."

"That squaw with 'im?"

"Yes, sir."

"When they get on the road tomorrow, I want you to go get her. Buy her, or just take her, I don't care which. Take a couple of men with you. I think I'd like to have her around; she shore is pretty. Besides, he owes us after cuttin' us out of the deal. "

"Yes, sir. And if he gives us trouble?"

"Do what you have to do."

CHAPTER 4

When they had ridden past the blacksmith shop, the last building on the street out of town, Daniel let Adam hold the reigns.

"Just hold them steady, Adam, right down the road."

"Okay, Pop, I got it."

It wasn't long before they were overtaken by three men on horseback, and Corky greeted them with barks. Daniel shook his finger at the dog and told him to hush. He minded Daniel most of the time, and this time he got quiet.

When they were even with the buckboard, one man spoke out loudly. "My boss seen yore squaw in town. He said she shore is purdy, and wants to know how much ya want fer her?"

"She's not for sale, go way! shouted Adam.

"Shut up, kid; I ain't talkin' to you."

Daniel spoke loudly but calmly. "You heard my son; now move on."

"You so chicken you let yore little boy speak fer you?"

"You heard me . . . move on."

"I reckin I can travel where I want to; they tell me it's a free country, ain't that right boys?" he said laughing toward the other men.

"It is, my friend, but I'm free to tell the sheriff I shot all three of you in self-defense."

"You talk big fer a feller that's out-numbered three to one.

"The odds seem about right to me."

"You're the one that interfered with our payday out west. Well, I think I'll just shoot you and take your squaw. Me and the boys ain't had no fun lately."

"All I can say is, you've been warned."

The man who had been talking moved his hand toward his gun saying, "We'll just see."

Daniel drew and shot him. As he fell from his horse, the others were taken by surprise. He had pulled his gun quickly and they were slow. That was their fatal mistake.

Unfortunately, Corky caught one of the men's stray bullets and died quickly. Adam pulled the dog into his arms with tears streaming down his face. "Pop, they killed Corky," he sobbed.

"I'm so sorry, son. We'll go down by the stream and give him a proper burial. When they had cared for Corky, they returned to take care of the three men.

Daniel had room on the back of the buckboard which had been extended to haul supplies to the hospital, so he loaded two of the men, tied their horses behind, then went to get the third man who had rolled down the hill across a large flat rock, marking it with blood as he rolled. He tied that horse with the others, and then turned the buckboard around and headed back into town to the sheriff's office.

When he arrived at the office, a sign identified the 'Sheriff's Office' and Brian Egelston as the sheriff.

Brian Egelston was in his late thirties, and had been elected sheriff five years ago, shortly after his departure from the Rangers. He was married and had a son about the same age as Adam.

Daniel stepped up on the board porch in front of the sheriff's office, and went in through the open door.

"Howdy, Sheriff; I ran into a little trouble just outside of town."

The sheriff rose and came around the desk. "Oh? What kind of trouble, Mister Fleming?"

"Thank you for remembering me, Sheriff. Some of the BZ boys, I think, upset because I interfered with their robbery the other day, wanted to buy my wife. When I said no, they pulled guns, and said they would take her anyway. As luck would have it, I guess I was a bit faster than they were."

"We've been having a lot of trouble with them. I guess it's a good thing you are leaving.

"John Holton brought them fellers in to steal a little land from the cattlemen around this area so as to homestead a ranch. I can't prove what he was doing was illegal, but it sure did raise a stink. Holton will be upset, but I'll handle Holton. You and your family can move on. Just watch out. You never know what'll be around the next corner."

"I thank you, Sheriff."

Daniel and the sheriff stepped outside in front of the office.

"These are the men and the horses they were riding."

"Don't you worry. I'll take care of them so that you can be on your way before Holton discovers what's happened. Daniel and Brian lifted the men onto the wooden walk under the shade provided by the overhang.

Daniel and his family were once again on their way.

After having traveled for quite some time on the hot and dusty trail, they came to a large group of oak trees and decided to stop. Daniel said, "It's getting too hot for us and the horses. We should stop under the shade of those trees until it cools a bit."

Daniel took the horses that were trailing behind the buckboard and the horse pulling the buckboard into the shade of the oak grove where there was a little grass growing. Jennifer spread the tarp so they could sit or nap until it cooled down a bit.

After about an hour, Adam said, "Pop, there's a rider coming fast."

"I see him, son. You and your mom move behind the buckboard."

Daniel walked to the edge of the shade and waited for the rider to approach.

When the man got close, he asked, "You the man who shot my cowboys?"

"If you're talkin' about the BZ boys, yes, I'm your man. You must be Holton."

Holton shouted, "So, you think you're fast just because you bush-wacked my men!"

"I'm afraid you have been misled if you think they were bush-wacked. Your men pulled iron when I told them to move along."

"I suppose next you'll say you out-drawed all three of them?"

"They were a bit slow. Did you ride out here to get shot, too?"

That upset Holton and he started to get off his horse.

"I'd stay mounted if I were you, Mister Holton. I've been as nice as I can be to you and your men; but if you get down, that places us on an even keel, and I won't have any sympathy left for you. So you need to stay on your horse and get back to the BZ to look for more hands. It's just too hot to bury you; I'll be forced to leave you for the buzzards, 'cause I'm not going back to town just to return the body of a hothead."

Holton was boiling mad, as Daniel taunted him. Holton obviously wasn't sure, but seemed to consider the fact that if this man out-drew three of his hands, he just might be very fast. He decided he did not want to take the chance. Reluctantly he reined his horse around and left hurriedly.

Daniel watched him a far piece down the trail, and then went back to sit in the shade.

"Boy, pop, you sure told him."

"No, son, I talked him out of committing suicide."

"What is that . . . suicide?"

"That, Adam, means killing one's self," said Jennifer.

Adam smiled and said, "Oh, I see."

"Well, it's beginning to cool a little, and we've a long way to get to the farm, so let's gather this stuff together and move on, at least for a while."

Once they started back on the trail, large white puffy clouds began to form and the trail became much more pleasant.

Adam caught up to Daniel and asked, "Pop, do you think it's gonna rain?"

"I don't think so, son. Those aren't the kind of clouds that hold a lot of water. See those away over on the horizon?"

"Yeah, they are kinda darker than these are. Does that mean they hold a lot of water?"

"Usually they do. If they move this way, we'll need to find shelter, son."

Jennifer gave a 'poof' through her lips and asked, "Just where do you expect to find shelter out here? You can't see anything but flat land for miles and it appears to be a desert."

"If the wind blows hard, we can get into one of those buffalo wallers," responded Daniel.

"And if it rains we will drown, because they fill quickly with water," Jennifer said as she raised her eyebrows.

"That's true. I see what might be trees a ways up the trail; but to get there, we will have to get off the trail and go a little south."

Jennifer wiped her brow with her handkerchief and said, "I could use a little shade right now."

They rode on toward what Daniel thought might be trees. Soon several appeared, along with a creek flowing clear water.

"This may be the best we can come up with, but I'll look around a bit just in case."

"This oak has a wide thick spread, so I guess if you don't find anything better, let me know and I'll start camp. No use riding in the rain," Jennifer commented while climbing down from the buckboard.

The sides of the creek had been cut by rushing water over the years, and the creek was deep in the sandstone. Daniel rode down into the creek looking for an overhang that might provide more protection in case of hail that often accompanied spring showers. Finding none, he returned to the tree where Adam and Jennifer were waiting.

"I guess this is the best we can do. There is plenty of good water in the creek, just a bit hard to get to. The creek is pretty deep.

"I'll go get water in the water bag, Pop,"

"Okay son, There's a big rock a ways down there and it will be easier to get down to the water there. Just be careful."

"I will."

Jennifer had started to set up camp, so Daniel joined her.

He smiled at her. "I didn't mean for you to have to go through all this."

Jennifer turned toward him. "I'm doing all right, Daniel. It's in my blood you know," she said with a little laugh.

"You know I love you very much?"

"I know, Daniel, and I love you, too."

Daniel kissed her on the cheek, and they proceeded to gather wood to build a fire to cook the evening meal.

Soon Adam returned with the water.

"What took you so long, Son?"

"There were some crawdads in the creek, and I tried to catch a few."

"Did you see any fish?"

"Nope, just crawdads is all. I haven't caught any yet, but I'm goin' back after we eat."

"Okay, just don't fall in, it's too far down there to come and get you out," he joked.

"Okay, I'll be careful."

They sat on the tarp and finished their evening meal. Adam went crawdading. Daniel and Jennifer sat back and finished their coffee.

"How far is it to headquarters, Daniel?"

"It will probably take two more days."

"Well, that's not too far, I guess."

Daniel saw Adam coming up from the creek. "Did you get any this time?"

"Yep, got a whole bunch!" he gleefully reported.

"Is there any water in your bucket, with the crawdads?"

"Enough to cover them."

"There are plenty of coals left, so just set the bucket over them. They'll boil pretty quick; we'll have them later."

Adam carefully placed the bucket on the coals so nothing would spill.

"I never did see any fish, but there could be some in there. I'll look some more later."

"Go before dark so you won't get lost."

"Aw, Pop, I won't get lost."

CHAPTER 5

When the camp was in near darkness, all three were in their sugans. Exhausted from the heat and work of the day, all were asleep almost immediately.

On a not too distant butte, three men had been watching them since early afternoon. When it was still light enough, they advanced on the camp. When it was almost so dark as to not be able to see, they moved into the camp, and the lead man, Holton, shot Daniel twice in his bed.

Jennifer, not knowing if the shots were a warning, or if one of the family was shot, remained in her sugan, but Adam jumped up to see what was going on.

Jennifer cautioned him quietly. "Adam, sit down, son." Even though it was almost dark, he could see the blood on Daniel's head.

"You've shot my Pop!" he started throwing punches at the only man he could make out in the dark. The man immediately back-handed him. Then Adam was too stunned to move. The man reached down and jerked Jennifer up with so much force it stripped off her blouse.

"This is what I came after. He wouldn't sell her, so I'll just take her. My, but you are a beautiful thing."

She scratched his face and kicked him hard.

"A feisty one! I like that. You'll be nice to have around the house."

"I'm not going with you; you'll have to kill me to get near me." Then she kicked him where it counted.

He slapped her. "Why you little . . ."

One of his men hissed, "Holton, let her go! I hear wagon chains rattling . . . someone's coming. Let's get out of here; they'll hang us if we get caught here."

John Holton raised his head and listened a moment. While his head was turned, Jennifer kicked him again in the groin. Angered, he shoved her down and shot her and Adam, too; then they ran for their horses and rode into the darkness.

The wagon slowly advanced. The folks in the wagon were not sure they had heard shooting since their wagon made so much noise. To see the trail and to find a camping place, a boy carried a lantern and walked in front of the wagon.

"You see anything, boy?" asked the old man on the wagon seat.

"Yeah, there's a camp up ahead, Grandpa."

"Well, hello the camp afore you walk in or they may shoot you," Grandpa warned.

"Hello the camp!" the boy yelled. No answer came. He advanced farther and held the lantern high while squinting to see. "They's three of 'em, Grandpa. They all been shot."

"Lord a mercy!" the old man exclaimed, "They all dead?" he asked.

"It shore looks like it," said the grandson."

The old man got off the wagon seat and moved toward the scene. "It's a whole family. I Reckon there's high-jackers around. Put that lantern behind that little tree, they'll be enough light fer us to see, and maybe they won't see us too well. Momma, you don't want to get down yet."

She peered into the darkness from the bonnet she was still wearing. "All right, Seth. You be careful; them shooters may still be around. I shore don't want you and the boy to get hurt and leave me out here alone."

The man began to examine each one. "This boy ain't over ten, and this here woman is part Indian, I'm shore. She shore was purdy. The man, he's . . ." he stopped talking. "He just moved. I believe he's still alive!" exclaimed Seth Granger as he lifted Daniel's head. "What happened here, Mister?"

Daniel barely opened his eyes; he haltingly managed to respond. "I don't know. I was sound asleep . . . the last thing I know is I heard a shot, then I was out, I guess. What about Jennifer and Adam?"

The old man didn't answer directly but said, "We need to get you to a doctor. You been shot twice, and you done lost enough blood to fill a dutch oven. Darrel, help me get this feller in his buckboard. It'll be faster than the wagon. We gotta get 'im to a doctor!"

They placed Daniel in his own buckboard. The boy looked at the horses and saw the harness sweat marks on one, and decided he was the one to hitch up.

"Darrel, we'll load the lady and boy in our wagon. You drive that buckboard as fast as you can back to Lubbock.

"Yes, Grandpa . . . Can you see all right? It's startin' to get a little light."

"I'm okay. Just get that man to the doctor."

"Yes, sir," responded the boy.

The boy popped the reins and the buckboard shot back up the trail.

As the buckboard passed the wagon, the old man shouted, "Darrel, don't run that poor horse to death!"

Seth Granger turned the wagon around, "Hold on momma, we're goin' back to town."

"I figgered as much," came Sarah's response. "I sure hate these two fine lookin' people cain't visit with us on the way back to town."

The Grangers had been living in Tucumcari, New Mexico, running a blacksmith shop. They were headed back to Tennessee to help out a daughter with her child who had disabilities.

Darrel Granger, their young grandson, had run the horse as long as he knew he should, so he pulled up, let the horse blow a bit, and then took him to water.

"Sorry we don't have time to graze, ole feller," he said while patting the horse's neck. "We gotta get this man to a doctor."

Darrel wet a piece of cloth he found in the buckboard, and bathed Daniel's face, wiping away some of the dried blood. Shortly he jumped onto the seat and was on his way again.

The sun was coming up when he pulled to a halt in front of the doctor's office. Dust rolled around the buckboard as he ran inside yelling for the doctor.

"Hold on young man. What's all the ruckus?"

"Quick, Doc! A man's been shot, and I had to bring him a long way to town. Please have a look."

Darrel and the doctor hurried to the buckboard where the doctor began to examine Daniel.

"This man has lost a lot of blood, but you got it stopped before he bled to death. Here, help me get him inside."

Daniel moaned and mumbled something they couldn't make out.

"Put him on the table by the window where there'll be more light. What's his name?"

The boy motioned for the doctor to step aside with him where he spoke quietly. "Doc, we don't know his name. His wife and son were shot too . . . but, we didn't tell him they was dead. We just told him they was in the wagon."

"Good Lord! You did the right thing I expect. Best he don't know for a while. It could have an effect on his recovery, if he *does* recover. I gotta get back to him," he said returning to Daniel's side.

"Doc, my grandpa and grandma are headed to the undertaker, so I reckon I'll go over there and help get those folks in the ground."

The doctor didn't respond as he was feverishly working to clean the wounds to get them bandaged to totally stop the bleeding.

Doctor Blanchard had taken care of Daniel as best he could. He put him in a clean, warm bed and Daniel was sleeping soundly, when there was a knock on the door.

"Come on in." The doctor stood from his seat as Seth Granger entered. "Howdy, doc. I'm Seth Granger. Me and the Mrs. and the boy found him and his family camped alongside the road. I don't know who he is, or whether he has any money; but if you need some to take care of him I'll have to bring it to ye later, cause I ain't got any right now."

"Don't you worry about it, Mister Granger. You've done your part; the rest is up to me and God."

"Thank you, doc, I hope you don't mind if my famly goes on about our snake killin'."

Doctor Blanchard knew just what he meant. "Yeah, you go ahead and take care of your business; I'll take care of this fellow."

"Thank you much, Doc."

As Seth was headed for the door, the doctor said, "Just so you know, Mister Granger, you probably saved this man's life."

CHAPTER 6

After Daniel's apparent recovery . . . *apparent*, because he could not remember who he was, or anything else of importance to his life, the doctor told him he believed it would be alright to leave the office. He had been there several weeks and felt it would be good for Daniel to get outside and move around.

Drying his hands, the doctor said, "I've told you about all I know about what happened to you, and by the way, the undertaker told me a while back that he had your stuff when you are ready to pick it up."

"My stuff, huh? Well, I guess I'd better go and rummage through it. Maybe it'll tell me who I am. He reached up to put on his hat. "Dang, doc, you cut all my hair off! My hat don't fit any more. How am I going to keep it on in the wind?"

Doc looked at him and chuckled. "Tie a piggin' string around it."

"Except for the haircut, I can't thank you enough, Doc, and as soon as I get some work, I'll pay you for all you were out taking care of me."

"We can worry about that another time," Doctor Blanchard said reassuringly.

Daniel left the doctor's office and headed to the undertaker's. He couldn't help noticing the hearse with its glass side windows as he walked in. *Sure glad I didn't have to ride in that*, he thought, and stepped up on the porch and knocked on the door.

The door was opened by a small man wearing small, round, gold-rimmed glasses. He had on a black suit, the skin on his face was drawn tight, and his eyes darted back and forth.

"May I help you?" he asked.

"Yes, sir, The doctor said you had my stuff, and said I could come pick it up."

"You're the one who was shot? Yes, yes, I'm Cyrus Banks, and I have it all here, but the horses are at the livery."

"Horses?"

"Yesser, three good-looking horses, and a buckboard. They are at the livery. Your other things are in my storage closet waiting for you."

"Was there anything in there that would tell me who I am?"

"I didn't touch anything, so I wouldn't know. You are welcome to spread it out in the store room if you like."

Dutch smiled. "I appreciate that, and I think I will. Oh, Mister Banks, do you know who brought me in?"

"A man named Seth Granger and his wife. I think the Grandson rushed you to the Doc's office. They've gone on to Tennessee, I think."

He went into the storage room and found three saddles and saddlebags. He picked the bags up first, dumped them out, and started shuffling through the contents.

He then saw a bag with draw strings. He picked it up, opened it, and then dumped it in the same manner as with the saddlebags. What fell out surprised him. He stared at a small metal plaque with the inscription: *Awarded to Daniel Fleming in grateful appreciation for saving the addition to our hospital.* It was signed by the board of directors. Digging farther into the bag, he found an envelope, which contained a check for Five Hundred Dollars which had apparently been presented to him with the plaque. He also found quite a few gold eagles and some smaller coins.

"Mister Banks, did you bury two others who were with me?"

"Yesser, we did. There are no names at the grave, because we did not know any."

"I can understand that because I've been in about the same shape.

"I'll have the money for their burial as soon as I go to the bank.

"The Sheriff said it was a woman and a boy, right?

"Yes, that's right, and Mister Granger said you were delirious, but you asked how a Jennifer and Adam were doing."

"I don't remember asking that, but If you would, I would like for you to make a third grave, as if we were all three there; place my name, Daniel Fleming on it. On the woman's put Jennifer, wife of, and on the boy's, put Adam, the son of. It seems I have lost my wife and a son that would have sired another generation of our family, but right now I don't remember either one.

"Hopefully someday I'll recover my memory and find the ones responsible for this. Until then I can't even grieve because they are all strangers to my mind. I am even a stranger to myself. I do hope that was their names, but I guess it doesn't matter until I can remember for sure. The third grave will cause whoever did this to be confident that no one will ever know. Then maybe they will let their guard down."

Daniel proceeded to the bank where he opened an account, took some cash, and then returned to the doctor's office.

"Doc, how much do I owe you for all you've done for me? I found I have the money to pay up."

"Since you are now a paying customer, seven dollars for the two weeks you were here ought to cover it. I wish I could have brought your memory back, but that will just take time."

"I understand, and thank you for saving my life. I know I nearly ran out of blood, but you pulled me through anyway."

"You are welcome; that's what I'm here for."

As the days passed, bits and pieces of memory flashed through his mind. Some stayed while others faded again. He walked the streets and stopped in at the livery.

"Name's Chester. What can I do fer ya?"

"I am told I have some horses here."

"And who be ye, sir? Chester inquired.

"Well, I was shot, the doc saved me and I don't rightly know who I am, but the doc says the horses are mine."

Chester grinned. "Yes sir, you do. Three of them, and dad gum good horses they are, too."

He saddled one horse knowing for some reason it was his, and then rode the plains for days just trying to get some hints of his former life.

When he returned to the livery, he saw the owner. "Chester, it's getting close to the end of the month. I probably have another livery bill to take care of, so you want me to square with you now or later?"

"If you're not thinking of leavin', just let it ride. Your bill's not too much anyway; a little grain is the most you owe for."

"Well, let me know when you want me to catch up, and I'll do it."

"That's fine . . . dang I don't know your name, have you thought of it yet?"

"According to what I've found, it's Daniel."

"That's good to know. A body ought'a know his name."

"I guess it fits me. When someone says that name, I get the feeling I ought to answer."

Daniel left the livery and headed to the boarding house for supper. The usual faces were already assembled at the long table. The owner, Grace Sewell, and the girls that were helping her, were skirting around bringing food to the tables. Daniel sat down by Floyd Timber, the general store owner.

"Floyd, is your wife still visiting her sister?"

"Yep; be home in a couple of days."

"I don't reckon you miss her cooking, since you have Grace to keep you fed?"

"No . . . but don't you tell Marie."

"Your secret is safe with me, Floyd."

"Grace, you and the girls have outdone yourselves tonight. This is quite a spread"

"Thank you; it's a special time. We have been here for ten years today!" she said proudly.

"Well, congratulations. You sure know how to celebrate."

Grace could have been a year or so older than Daniel, but he couldn't tell for sure. She had blue eyes, red hair and a body far more beautiful than any of the young girls she had working for her in the dining room.

After supper when the girls were cleaning up for Grace, she stopped Daniel in the lobby of the boarding house.

"Have you made any progress about your past, yet?"

"No, not since I found out my name. By the way, it seems to be Daniel Fleming.

"Daniel Fleming . . . I like it!" she said smiling.

"As for progress, I have strange thoughts occasionally drifting through my mind, but so far nothing that sticks, and nothing that gives me a serious clue. I learned my wife's name was Jennifer and my son's was Adam." He started to turn, thought a minute, and then he asked, "Grace, do you ride?"

"Sure do. Been riding since I was a kid."

"I know you know how, I was wondering if you still do."

"I do. Why?"

"I thought, since it's your anniversary, you might like to go for a ride in the cool of the evening. It might help if I had a beautiful lady to ride with me. I know my wife must have ridden with me because we were riding when I was shot. Maybe you will trigger some memory."

"Oh, so you want to use me, do you?"

"No. As I said, I want a beautiful woman by my side. Just a short ride; it will be dark soon."

"I'd like that Daniel, but I don't have a horse."

"You can't get out of it that easy, Grace. I have an extra horse and saddle. I'm sure it's a gentle horse because my former wife rode it, or the boy did . . . not sure which."

"Let me change and I'll be right with you," she said.

When she reappeared, Daniel's eyes widened. "Wow, you look great!" he said.

"Oh, meaning I didn't look great before?"

"No! Oh, I didn't mean it that way. I just mean, oh, heck you know what I mean."

"I do know," she said smiling. "Let's get going; it won't get any earlier."

CHAPTER 7

At the livery stable, Latigo, Daniel's horse nickered and moved toward him. His other two horses followed closely. They seem to know him by their actions. He didn't know his horses name was Latigo, though.

"Boy, you have them trained well since they come before you even call."

"They probably think I'm going to feed them. I just wish I could remember their names."

"I doubt they are thinking of feed. They show love, the way they nicker and push against you. It must be frustrating to not be able to call them by name."

"It is for sure." Daniel saddled her horse first, helped her on, and then saddled Latigo. Daniel felt she might be more comfortable if they left from behind the livery instead of riding through town.

Noticing his backdoor exit she asked, "Why did you go this way? Are you ashamed to be seen riding with me?"

"Not at all! I just thought you might be more comfortable going this way."

"That's sweet, Daniel, but I don't mind, *or care* for that matter, who sees what I do or with whom I do it."

"Thank you, Grace. I really like your calling me by name."

"And Im glad you have a name now to be called by. Even though I wondered about that line of yours 'helping with your memory'."

They rode for a while until Daniel said, "I think it's better if I don't ride by myself. I don't know why . . . It's just a feeling. Thank you for making that possible."

"No problem. I like to ride," she responded.

"I have these flashes of memory but they don't mean anything to me."

"When you got the award for saving the hospital money, I was there, Daniel. I saw your wife and son that day."

"You were there?"

"Yes."

"No one else has told me that. It's like everybody has forgotten."

"Not me. Your wife looked Indian. She was beautiful."

"She was Cherokee. I found her in Oklahoma," he said, and immediately realized that it was a memory he did not have before.

Startled, he turned to Grace. "You see. You do help me remember! Now, if I can only remember why I was in Oklahoma."

"It will just take time, Dan; looks like you will remember everything, soon."

"I like being called Dan. That's what my folks called me. It seems more relaxed than Daniel. You see, Grace, you do have a special way of helping. You triggered memories from a long time ago that the folks called me Dan," she smiled in response.

"I'd like to ask you to ride again soon, Grace. I think you make a lot of difference."

"Any time I'm not tied down with the boarding house."

"That seems to take a lot of your time."

"I have help, and if it's not too busy I can get away for a while."

"I can't thank you enough, Grace. I want you to know I'm not doing this as a ploy to be with you, I sincerely think it will help; however, I'm growing to like you very much since I've been staying at the boarding house."

"I've been glad to have you, Dan."

"We should probably head back now."

She nodded in agreement and they turned and headed back to the livery stables.

Daniel unsaddled the horses and Grace helped him rub them down. She commented, "I really like this horse, Dan."

"Well, consider him yours when you need a horse. They will be here, and the saddles, too."

"Thank you, Dan."

"What's the menu tonight, Grace?"

"I think they have put together a nice meatloaf."

"That sounds quite tasty. I'll see you then."

Daniel went to his room to wash up and Grace went to the kitchen.

Georgia Baker, the cook, spoke to Grace when she came into the kitchen. "You know that man's sweet on you, don't you, Grace?"

"I don't know, Georgia; he just needs help to remember."

"Yeah, he gonna remember his way right into your heart. I knows what I'm talkin' about.

Grace laughed.

"You think what you want, honey, I watch that man when you move around where he is."

Grace bit her lower lip, "I don't guess that's a bad thing, Georgia; he is a very handsome man."

"Yesum, I reckon he is for a white man."

"How's the meatloaf doing, Georgia?"

"Now you can change tha subject if you wants to, but that man is sweet on you . . . you'll see."

After the meal, Daniel moved to the porch where a swing was hung for those who stayed at the boarding house. He was enjoying the cool breeze that came in after the sunset. Soon, Grace came out of the front door.

She saw him sitting in the swing, smiled and said, "I heard you were sitting out here."

"Enjoying the cool breeze. Have a seat if you have time."

"I do have a bit of time. It really is cool."

"I ordered it special, because I knew you'd be out soon."

"Oh, you did, did you?"

"Yes'um, I surely did."

"You know, Dan, I've not set in this swing before."

"You mean you've been here ten years and haven't set in this swing until tonight?"

"That's right."

"That makes me feel kinda special. Maybe there's a chance of getting you to do other things you've never done before."

"Now Dan, I hope you mean things like sittin' in a swing or washing down a horse!"

"I see what you mean. I really didn't mean to imply anything shady, Grace. I'm talkin' about things like helping me remember by doing things neither of us have done.

"Maybe you can tell me more about my family, since you were there the day of the reward."

"Well . . . I remember when the hospital director offered you his buckboard; your wife stepped forward and thanked him after you did. You took the pack off of a horse and hooked him to the buckboard. After that everybody left. I did too. That's about what I remember. Oh, yes. She was wearing a red skirt and a yellow blouse . . . and her hair was pulled back into a pony tail. Does that ring a bell for you?"

Daniel rubbed his chin, and then looked up at Grace. "Nothing's coming to mind. Maybe this isn't the way to go about it, Grace."

"Give it time, Dan; it'll come to you sooner or later."

"I hope so. My brain may be damaged worse than we thought."

"Your brain seems to be doing everything else all right, Dan."

"I guess so. I think I'll go ride old Latigo a while."

Grace looked surprised. "Ride who, Dan?

"I said Latigo . . . I don't know why."

"Because that's your horse's name, I'll bet! You've been trying too hard, Dan. Just let it go on it's on, and maybe it'll come to you little by little."

"Are you still going to ride with me tomorrow, Grace?"

"Are you still going to church with me tomorrow?"

"Yes I promised I would."

"Well, then, I'll have some lunch prepared, and we can stop by the lake and picnic under the willows."

"That sounds great, Grace." He turned toward her looking down at his shirt. "I'll need to get something to wear; can't wear these to church."

Daniel met Grace at the office of the boarding house early the next morning.

"Grace, you look so beautiful this morning."

"Well, thank you, Dan, you look pretty good yourself. We can stop by here after church and pick up our lunch."

"I hooked up the buckboard this morning . . . I wouldn't want that pretty dress to get messed up."

After the sermon the, preacher stood in the pulpit and spoke to the congregation. "Most of you folks have met the man that has lost his memory, Daniel Fleming, and know that he has had trouble recalling his previous life. Let's join together in prayer for that to change.

"Oh Lord in heaven, we've gathered together today to worship you, knowing that you are in charge of all things. You are all knowing, Father, and we pray that you might restore memory to our brother Daniel Fleming that he might know a bit more about his previous life, so that he can take care of anything that might be lacking to be done. Go with us as we leave here today, we pray in Jesus name."

Most of the folks shook Daniel's hand, and called him by name, as they stood in front of the building until he and Grace finally managed to get away. They got in the buckboard and stopped to pick up their lunch, then headed out of town to the lake.

After they selected a place to spread the tarp where they could sit in the shade and have their lunch, Grace sat down while Daniel gathered wood to build a fire to make coffee.

"This gentle breeze out of the south should carry the smoke away from us."

"I hope so; I'll smell it all night if I get too much."

"I'm sorry . . . we can pass on the coffee if you had rather."

"No, coffee is fine; the breeze is carrying it away in the opposite direction."

Daniel stared into the fire and was silent.

"What are you thinking, Dan?"

"I was just wondering . . . why do I remember how to saddle a horse, light a fire, put on my pants, for that matter, and can't remember who I am, where I came from, or who with?"

"Dan," she said as she took his hand. "You're trying too hard . . . let it come as it will."

Daniel smiled at Grace. "I'm trying to, Grace, but sometimes I just wonder about things."

"Let's just eat and enjoy the breeze. It' a beautiful Sunday; we should enjoy it."

"I am enjoying it, Grace. Just being with you makes me realize I don't really need to remember anything....just enjoy it."

"Now you're getting the idea, Dan." She stood up. "I'll get us another sandwich."

Daniel rose quickly and said, "Let me get it, Grace."

As they stood face to face, Daniel stared into her blue eyes. They were motionless gazing into each other's eyes. Grace eased toward Daniel, and he followed through, meeting her half way with a long kiss.

Daniel backed up and apologized, "I'm sorry, Grace . . . I just couldn't resist. You are a beautiful lady; and I am being too forward."

"Dan, I wanted you to kiss me. I've wanted it ever since we started riding together."

"I'm glad, Grace. I've wanted to kiss you since I met you."

"Okay, now that we have that settled, let's finish eating."

With new sandwiches in hand, they settled on the blanket. "Where are you from, Grace? You haven't lived around here all your life have you?"

"Goodness, no. My folks moved us from Arizona to El Paso years ago. My dad went there to work for a land company, and my mom worked in a boot making shop. My cousin lived here and I visited her many times. She owned the boarding house, and when she died, she had no one else, so she left the place to me. I've been here ever since."

"I take it that was ten years ago," he stated.

"My-oh-my, but aren't you perceptive, since here we are celebrating my tenth year here," she said teasingly.

"I'm sorry, Grace, that really did just slip my mind."

"Well, don't let it happen again," she joked.

"You know, you make it hard to keep anything but you on my mind." he pulled her close and kissed her again.

"What are we going to do, Dan? It's probably too soon after your wife's death to go public."

"I suppose so," he agreed, "but I have no recollection of before, so it doesn't seem to register that it's too soon."

"We can let it be our secret for a while longer."

"Sure, that's what we ought to do . . . but I don't know how long we should wait, when I don't want to wait at all."

"I know. I feel the same way. Do you have any idea what kind of work you did previously?"

"I'm afraid not. I suppose I was just a cowhand."

"Why don't you check on some of the ranches around here, to see if you can get work? That ought to take your mind off of this terrible situation you are in, and maybe your memory will come to you once you apply your mind to something else."

"You make a lot of sense, Grace. I guess I'm not thinking straight.

CHAPTER 8

Daniel was in the mercantile shopping for a new shirt when he heard a loud commotion that seemed to be taking place near the saloon. He walked to the front door to see what was happening. Jacob Higgindorf, the proprietor of the mercantile, was standing outside watching.

"What's goin' on, Jacob?" asked Daniel.

"A couple of the BZ guys are having it out. They do this often. Don't know why Holton won't hire people that git along . . . but he don't. They are all gun handlers, I hear."

Daniel squeezed his eyebrows together. "BZ? I've heard that before.

"Yeah, John Holton runs it. It's out north of town. He cut it out of land that belongs to the XIT, but they haven't done anything about it yet."

"Jacob, you are hitting parts of my memory. The BZ, and the name John Holton. Seems as if I've heard of them before. They are not very pleasant memories as near as I can tell."

"Well, what can I do for you, Daniel?"

"I came for a new shirt. At least I can remember what I came in here for," he chuckled.

"Daniel, I got a shipment I haven't put out yet. Let's go in the back and I'll show them to you."

"I'm with you; let's look," agreed Daniel as they headed to the back of the store.

"They are made of Egyptian cotton. Supposed to be a hitch better than our cotton here in the states, so they tell me, and easier to take care of."

Daniel smiled at Jacob. "Between you and me, I think that's hog wash!"

"Now be careful, Daniel. The ladies around here swear by it. They tell me it irons easier and feels better. Not as scratchy. They ought to be better. I have to charge a whole dollar for them!"

"Don't tell the ladies I said so, but like I said, it's hog wash. 'Course I ain't never tried to iron a shirt. I sure like the looks of these, but I think I better stick to the fifty cent ones."

"Grace will like it, Daniel."

"What do you mean, Jacob?"

"I been watchin' you two a comin' and goin' for some time now. I got an idea you two just may wind up as one."

"Actually, we just ride together so's I can get my memory back."

"Sure, you can tell folks that if you want to, but Grace hasn't been that close to no man for the last ten years. This feller Holton, I hear, has wanted to court her, but she won't have anything to do with him."

"Well, you just tell folks she's just helping me recover my memory. I don't want to start any rumors that would embarrass her in any way. You really think she would like this new kind of shirt?

"Yesser, I sure do," he replied grinning.

Daniel picked the shirt he liked best and headed to the door. "Thanks for the shirt, Jacob. Just put it on my bill. I'll come by tomorrow and tell you if it feels any better than my old shirt."

That evening after supper was finished, Daniel mentioned to Grace the argument in front of the saloon today.

"That's something that happens often with that BZ bunch of John Holton's when they are in town. They get drunk and then fight each other."

"That's what Jacob said, but the BZ and the name John Holton struck a chord in my mind; other names haven't done that. I've got something in my brain that was set off when I heard them. Don't know why yet, but I'll keep it revolving around in there until it makes sense."

"Jacob said Holton had his eye on you."

She rolled her eyes. "He can keep on wishing, but it's not going to happen."

"I'll not ask you to waste time with me tonight, I think I'll ride alone."

"Dan, I don't mind riding with you, and it's not a waste of time, besides it nearly dark now."

"I know, but where I'm going to ride the trail is sand and it shows up in the dark. I've traveled it before."

Puzzled at his comment, she said, "Okay then, I'll see you in the morning at breakfast."

Daniel headed north out of town, which happened to be the trail where all his trouble began. The trail was easily followed, because even though the sun had gone down the twilight was plenty to see the terrain along the trail.

When he had reached the place of the first encounter with Holton, Latigo stopped.

"What's the matter, Latigo? Do you see something I can't? . . . or do you hear something I don't hear?"

He got off his horse, examined his hooves, looked around but nothing he could discover seemed to be the reason the horse had stopped.

Daniel dropped the reins, and started walking around. "Latigo, have we been here before?" he asked softly. He wandered all around trying to solve the mystery in his mind, until he came to a big flat rock. It had dark streaks across it, as if blood had dribbled as someone rolled across it.

He stared at it for a long time.

"Latigo, there's something familiar here, but it's too dark to see. Let's go back for now and come back tomorrow in the daylight. Then maybe something will pop into my head."

At breakfast the next morning, Daniel ordered his favorite before Grace came into the dining room. As he was eating, Grace came in and sat down beside him.

"Did you have a good ride last night?"

"Strangest thing happened, Grace. As we rode on the trail north, all of a sudden Latigo just stopped and stood there. I don't know if he sensed something or just got tired. Anyway, I got off and looked around a while and came across a large rock that looked as if it had blood smeared across it. I had a feeling maybe I rolled across it when I was shot, or someone else had. It was really too dark to determine, so I'll have to go out while the sun is shining to make sure it really was blood I saw."

"I'll go with you when you get ready to go."

"Thank you again, Grace. I hope I'm not taking you away from your business too much."

"You let me worry about that, Dan. I feel like I'm part of this mystery now, and I'm ready to help solve it."

At Grace's insistence, they decided to leave in the early afternoon. Daniel saddled the two horses, and by the time he was finished Grace came to the livery, ready to go.

They rode the trail north of town. When they had ridden to the place where Daniel had seen the rock, he stopped and dismounted. When Grace saw Daniel get down, she too stepped down and joined him by the rock.

"That's blood all right, Dan."

"I was sure it was last night, and you can see how it looks as if someone rolled across it."

"It does, Dan, but you were in your bed when you were shot, according to what the man who found you said."

"Hum. I hadn't thought of that. You see, Grace, I do need your help."

She stepped close to the rock to examine it. "It is blood all right and you can tell it was from someone rolling over it. See, a spot here, then a blank space, and then another matching spot, but it can't be yours. This isn't where you were found. I think your camp was further down the trail."

'You know where it was?"

"Yes, the general direction was pointed out to me one day after you were out of the doctor's office. I was headed out to Elizabeth's place."

"Can you show me where it is, Grace? Nobody ever told me."

"Yes, let's ride on further."

They mounted and rode north up the trail.

"Are you sure you want to do this, Dan?"

"I'm sure."

They rode for a while until Grace saw the trees where Daniel and his family might have camped. "This might have been the place...in the trees."

They stopped and stepped down to walk around the area. Daniel hoped that this would jog his memory.

"Close your eyes, Dan" He did so and stood facing the trees. He turned each direction as if he was surveying the area but with his eyes closed.

"What do you see, Dan?"

"Nothing, I have my eyes closed!"

She swatted his arm and laughed. "I mean what does your mind's eye see?"

"Nothing here, but back at the rock I now remember I shot a man off his horse and he did roll across that rock. But I don't know why I shot him."

"Well, since there is no body around here, why don't we go ask the sheriff if someone brought a shooting victim in to his office . . . other than you, of course?"

They mounted and rode back to town to visit with the sheriff.

Dropping their reins across the hitching rack, Grace entered the office before Daniel got the cinches loosened.

"Hello, Sheriff."

"Well, hello, Grace. What brings you here?"

"I brought Daniel Fleming to ask a question, Sheriff."

Daniel walked in and the sheriff greeted him. "How you been getting along? You had it pretty bad there for a while."

"Physically, I'm better, thanks. Not sure about mentally. I still can't remember much. I wanted to ask if any gunshot victims had been brought to you. I think I might have shot someone out on the trail."

"Well, son, the ones who found you asked me to kinda hold back on telling you much about what happened. They were a bit afraid to say much. They thought it might scramble things even worse, but I speck it's all right to say something now."

"So, you did find someone shot?"

"I didn't **find** . . . you brought 'em to me."

A little astonished Daniel said, "**I** brought them to you?"

"You sure did. They were three of 'em. They stopped you on the trail, tried to buy your wife, and when you told them no, they drew on you and you shot all three. Two of them right out of the saddle. They were BZ boys, kinda hired guns for Holton. After you dropped them off here, you headed on north towards the XIT ranch. Said you was s'posed to take on one of the farms for them."

"So, I wasn't just wandering. I had a job to go to. Guess that opportunity is long gone now."

Daniel and Grace headed back to the livery to drop off the horses. Once there, they rubbed them down, gave them some feed, then headed to the boarding house.

As they walked along, birds sang and children were playing, and a cool breeze kissed their cheeks. Dan looked at Grace. "Well, Grace, we found out a lot today. Now if I can fit it all together, won't that be somethin'?"

"It will, Dan. It will," she said, her eyes filling with tears.

"Grace, I think I'll get a shave and a bath before supper. I might better go tell the folks at the XIT why I didn't report when I was supposed to."

"That sounds like the right thing to do. Do you want me to ride there with you?"

"No, Grace. I'll go in the morning. And it's too far. I'll just go and be back pretty quick if I ride hard and long. I'll take two horses to let ole Latigo have a rest once in a while. But, you might get Georgia to put together a pack of her fine cooking so's I can survive until I get back."

CHAPTER 9

Early the next morning Daniel headed north once again, but this time to the offices of the massive XIT ranch, the largest ranch, under fence in the world. He only stopped to let the horses drink from water caught in a large buffalo wallow. The grass nearby was a mixture of side oats grama and buffalo grass. It was tall and in good shape for a lot of cattle. His horses enjoyed it, too, during his stop.

After a brief rest for him and his horses, Daniel rode on to the headquarters. When he arrived at the group of buildings, he rode to the Escarbada Bunkhouse where he saw a few cowboys on the porch.

"Howdy. I'm lookin' for the General Offices; can you help me?"

One of the hands standing at the edge of the porch pointed in the general direction of a little red house across the way. "That's the office yonder."

Tipping his hat in thanks, Daniel turned his horse toward the house. He dropped his reins as he dismounted, knowing Latigo would remain in that spot until he returned. The other horse was tied to the back of the saddle so he wouldn't go anywhere.

There were two entrances to the house. Not knowing which to take, he walked up the steps and went to the door that looked like it might be the main one and knocked.

"Walk on in," came a loud voice from within. "We don't knock around here." The man who bid him come in introduced himself as the foreman of the XIT, Charles Clement.

Daniel started to introduce himself, "Howdy, I'm," the man behind the desk cut him off.

"I know who you are! Daniel Fleming!"

"Yes, sir, that's me."

"Well, Daniel, you're a little late."

"Yes, sir, I had a little trouble, and I thought I'd come and tell you about it." Daniel explained what happened to him. "I thought I owed you an explanation."

"I'm sure sorry about your family. I guess you figgered we'd already hired someone for that job."

"Yes, sir, I did, and I can't blame you; it was just an unfortunate situation. After you and I talked in Colorado, I headed this way. After I was shot, I wasn't able to remember anything, and still don't remember much. The Sheriff told me I had mentioned I was headed here."

"Where are you staying, Daniel?"

"Right now at the boarding house in Lubbock."

"Well, if anything comes up, I'll try to contact you first."

"I appreciate that, Charles, and I thank you for the consideration."

"You're welcome. You just as well stay for supper. We feed everybody around five thirty."

"Well, since it'll get dark on me anyway, it won't hurt to start a little later. Thanks, I believe I will."

"Glad to have you. It's close to that time now, so let's head on over."

Together they walked by the large round pen where horses were fed. A large tin barn stood at one side of the pen. One of the hands was opening the door to get feed. The rattling of the chain, as he opened the door, sent out the news that grain was going to be dropped. As he filled the feed boxes for each horse, wild turkeys came running to the pen to scavenge any dropped grain. "Everyday occurrence," commented the man who was dropping the grain.

They continued to the kitchen where all the cowboys at headquarters were gathered.

"Boys, this is Daniel Fleming, **he thinks**. He was shot in the head and hasn't got his memory back, so we're going to fill him up afore he heads back to Lubbock. Sit down, Daniel, let's eat."

Like most ranches, they had several kinds of meat, from beef to venison, lots of potatoes and gravy with plenty of coffee and a plate full of biscuits.

They talked about farming and how many of the things they grew were actually used on the ranch, such as feed, hay, and then mentioned what they sold to other ranches.

During the conversation Daniel said, "I've heard that a fellow named Holton has cut out a chunk of the XIT and is calling it his own. What do you know about that, Charles?"

"Yeah, we know about it; just haven't got around to taking care of it yet. It's in the works. He's messing not only with us and our property, but with the State of Texas!" The other hands all nodded and muttered in agreement.

"I keep hearing about him and his people and it always makes me feel edgy. Seems like I should know what makes me feel that way, but at this point, I don't know what or why. I may look into it when I get back," said Daniel.

"If you and the sheriff there can do anything to get him out of the way, it will save us a lot of trouble."

"Boy! I'm not sure my horse will be able to carry me after a meal like that. Thanks again, and it was good to meet all you hard workin' hands." That got a laugh from the boys.

Daniel tightened the cinches on the horses, mounted up and headed back to Lubbock. The sun was low in the sky; but he could make a lot of miles before having to make camp.

When he did make a camp, he was once again lucky enough to find a buffalo wallow that still had good water in it from a recent rain. He watered the horses, picketed them and started a fire with dry grass and buffalo chips to make the coffee.

The sun painted a beautiful sunset of all colors ranging from gold to pink. He gazed toward it and was frozen in thought.

I have bits and pieces, but can't seem to put them together. Why can't I remember all of it? Why can't I remember my wife...my son?

When the sun dropped below the horizon, he turned toward the fire and poured another cup of coffee.

His thoughts moved to Grace Sewell. *Grace has been such a God-send, helping me in so many ways. I didn't realize how much I would miss her on this trip. I may not go anywhere without her again. Of course, that's only if she wants to ride along. I guess I can only hope at this point. She may not want to carry on very long with a guy who has no idea who, what, or **if** he'll ever know who he is.* He finished his coffee, carefully put out the fire, slipped into his sugan, and was soon asleep.

He was up before the sun, ate his breakfast and was in the saddle before the sky burst forth with a golden sunrise.

Within an hour, the wind picked up out of the northwest and the sky began to turn red with dust.

"Uh-oh! Looks like a sand storm coming, Latigo. I'm sure glad I took care of my fire this morning. In this wind, it could burn every pasture all the way to Kansas." He stopped and dismounted. He wanted to stay ahead of the storm, so he hurriedly took one of his old shirts from his saddle bag, ripped it in two, and made eye covers for both horses. The half shirt was long enough to cover their nostrils, and then he poured water from his canteen over the shirt to keep the sand out of their noses.

"You're gonna need that soon if the sand blows as hard as usual." He turned both horses' tails to the wind and picketed them. He tied his handkerchief around his own face, crawled into his sugan, and covered his head.

When he decided the storm had passed, he had no idea how long the wind and sand had blown, but his sugan was covered. He checked his horses, poured more water on the shirt parts and wiped out the nostrils of both horses.

"Looks like we survived another obstacle well enough to get on home." He broke camp, mounted and rode on toward Lubbock. He stopped at the first water he came to and washed out the horses nostrils again, then filled his canteen.

When he returned to the livery in town, Chester asked, "Where were you when that storm hit?

"I was in my sugan. It kept me from getting buried, but didn't protect completely. I need a bath mighty bad."

"You head on out, Daniel, I'll take care of the horses. That's what you pay me for. They look like they need a lot of brushin' and you DO need a bath!"

"Am I that dirty?"

"You sure are. You are as brown as Hurly over at the blacksmith shop."

"Thanks, Chester."

Daniel got his bath and shaved, put on his new shirt, and went to the dining room to eat. When he arrived at the dining hall, Grace walked by his table, carrying food, and commented, "Daniel I like your new shirt!"

"Jacob said you would," he replied.

She smiled and said, "He has good taste."

It was late when Daniel had gotten to the boarding house because he had taken his time cleaning up. Customers had slacked off, so Grace joined him at his table.

"How did your meeting at the XIT go?"

"It went well. Charles Clement, the foreman who had hired me to begin with, explained he had to hire someone for the farm when I didn't show up. I can't fault him for that."

"Did you ask him if he knew about Holton squatting on part of the ranch?" she asked.

"Yes, I did. He said he knew about it, but hadn't gotten around to taking care of it...yet. I told him I would check on Holton and his plans from this end."

"But what can you do alone, Dan?"

"Well, I thought I'd ride out and observe a while. I have some good glasses to watch from a distance."

"Oh, Dan, do be careful. Those men are known gun hands."

"Something else, Grace . . . on the way back I told myself I wouldn't ride again without you at my side, but I don't think it would be a good idea this time."

"That's sweet of you, Dan. I'll remember you said that."

"I know it will be best if I'm alone this time."

"I understand, but I'll miss you."

"And I'll miss you, too, but I need to sort things out."

"Dan, take all the time you need."

"Maybe I could call on Georgia to fix up a little of her specials to carry along. Tell her I really enjoyed the last one she fixed."

Grace smiled teasingly. "I'm sure she will be glad to. I think she may have a thing for you," he smiled approval.

Daniel went to his room to put together things he would need for a day or two on the trail as Grace returned back to the kitchen.

"Georgia, Dan would like for you to fix up some of your specialties for him. He is going to be gone a few days out on the trail."

Georgia smiled. "I tells you that man does have a crush on you, and I'as thinking that you done slipped in line with that same idea."

Grace turned so Georgia couldn't see her face as she blushed, and said, "Georgia, he is just lonely. He has lost his wife and child."

"Honey, he don't know that, he just been told that, by folks that are strangers. When he wakes up, you gonna be there, and he gonna know you been there all along for him. He for shore ain't forgettin' you, honey. Now set yo'self of a mind; 'sides, honey, you ain't getting' any younger. He da one for you!"

"I've about come to the same conclusions as you have, Georgia, but I don't want to push him too hard."

"Honey, if you don't push, some other gal is just likely to."

"I'll take all of this into consideration; now let's get this mess cleaned up for breakfast."

CHAPTER 10

Daniel left before dawn on Latigo and leading the pack horse, whose name he doesn't know, to spend time observing the BZ ranch and the man called Holton.

As light began to slowly show in the east, he saw heavy clouds starting to form. The wind started to blow harder and he felt moisture forming on his face.

"Latigo, we've got to find shelter. This time of year a cloud could produce hail, and if it does, we won't last long. Boy, if it's not a dust storm it's a rain storm. Why can't nature let things go right for a while?"

He searched for a tree large enough to offer a bit of shelter for himself and the horses, without much luck. Trees are scarce on the Llano Estacado. As it became lighter, he rode through a rocky creek bottom, where both large and small rocks lined the banks of high slabs of sandstone.

As he rounded a turn in the rift, he spotted a small cabin built out of the very stone he was riding through. It was a neat cabin carefully built with every stone fitted in place. Out back was a small barn with a corral at the side.

He rode close to the door and hailed to anyone who might be inside. "Hello the house!"

Soon the door opened and Daniel made his plea. "Can we take shelter from the storm in your barn?"

"Si, señor. En mi casa; put up your horses and come inside."

Daniel took the horses into the barn. The horses were reluctant to go into the dark barn with the flashes of lightning and thunder, but Daniel talked to them both, and they finally settled down. He loosened the cinches and removed their loads, rubbed them down, found some grain and hay, and gave them plenty to take their minds off of the storm. When he had finished, he went to the house, knocked and was admitted quickly.

The man holding the door was an older man of Mexican descent. His hair was totally grey, as was his heavy mustache; his dark eyes were smiling as he invited Daniel into his home.

"Muchas gracious," said Daniel as he entered. "Not only is it wet out there, but it's getting cold. My name is Daniel Fleming."

"I am Roberto Gonzales. You have come far?"

"I've come from Lubbock."

"Oh, that's not too far. But enough talk. The coffee is fresh and hot."

"Thank you very much. That'll hit the spot. You have a very beautiful home here."

"Si, I build myself," he said as he took a cup from the cabinet and poured steaming coffee into it.

"Well, you've done a wonderful job."

"Thank you. I'm trying to make my English better by speaking as much as I can, but I have no one to speak with. I am very glad you are here."

"You're doing very well in the English department, and believe me, I too am glad you are here. I'm not sure how bad that storm might get. Are you on the XIT?"

"No, my home is outside their ranch. When I was sent to build it, it was thought to be on the ranch; but after it was built, and when surveyed again, it was just outside; but it was still used as a line camp. I was to stay here, and to main . . . main..."

"Maintain it?" Daniel added.

"Si, ah, yes! Maintain it. The ranch sent me supplies and I cooked and everything else for them, and the cowboys would stay here when working this side of the ranch, and I still do if they come. There are several beds in the back room. That is where you can put you things."

"I'll do that in a minute. I just want to sit and slowly enjoy your good coffee. It is <u>very</u> good."

"My wife, Olivia, died a few months ago, and I have been alone here. But I don't mind; I find plenty to do."

"I'm sorry about your wife, Roberto." He paused and took another sip of coffee. "Can I ask you a question?"

"Si, what do you need to know?"

"There is a ranch that has been cut out of the XIT, by . . . "

"The BZ . . . John Holton," Roberto finished for him. "Si, I know of it."

"Have you ever observed what they do over there?"

"No señior, I am afraid to go close. One time I ride close to there, but they shoot at me. I stay away."

"I can't blame you."

"Do you plan to go there?" Roberto asked.

"No, I want to observe what is going on. Are there places where me and my horse can be out of sight to just watch them?"

"Si, there are boulders of, what you call them? . . . What the house is made of?"

"Sandstone?"

"Si, sandstone, on a hill so you can look down in the valley below."

"I thank you, Roberto, you've helped a lot."

"I have warm beans and some ham fried up. Would you like?"

"That would hit the spot, and maybe a little more coffee."

"Si, I have plenty."

"How long have you lived here, Roberto?"

"About forty years this spring. I guess you could say they retired me; but they still send some supplies, and I cook if any cowboys come this far. They gave me the house when I retired. I thought that was good."

"Yes, it was very good of them. Roberto, I plan to spy on the BZ for Mister Clement; not sure I'll find out anything, but I'm going to look. I think I have some sort of connection with it, or John Holton. I'm not sure."

"If you don't mind, señior, I would like to go with you. It gets kinda boring around here day after day, and your work sounds muy exciting. I know the land like the back of the hand; I could be useful."

Daniel sat a moment saying nothing. "That might be a good idea. When the rain stops, we'll give it a try. You do have a horse to ride?"

"Si, he is in pasture. I whistle, he comes."

"I've picked out a bunk, so I'll see you in the morning. By the way, thanks for the chow."

"De nada, señior. Good night."

 "Si, bueno noche.

Daniel and Roberto left before daylight, since the rain had stopped. As near as they could tell, it would stay clear.

It was only about three miles to the edge of the BZ and the overlook that Roberto had mentioned. When he saw what Roberto described, he said, "You were right . . . this is a perfect spot" He removed his field glasses from his saddlebags and moved up behind a large slab of sandstone turned up by a violent upheaval in eons past.

"Take a look, Roberto," he handed the glasses to him. "They seem to be branding, don't they?"

"Si, Señior that is what they are doing."

"I can't help but wonder if they are some he has raised or if the stock is XITs."

"It does make you wonder, Señior," Roberto agreed.

"Well, there's no way to tell from here. I might just ride in there to see."

"But, Señior, didn't you say they may be the ones who shot you?"

"Yes, they could be the ones . . . I'm not sure . . . I just can't remember."

"Then I will go. These men are not the ones that shot at me. They have seen me before and know where I live. They have even eaten at my home. I will be all right."

"Thank you, Roberto. Don't take any chances. I'll watch you from here with the glasses; just don't go behind buildings where I can't see you."

Roberto mounted and rode down to the corral. "Buenos días Señiors!" he greeted.

"Well, Roberto! Been a long time since you been by," one cowboy commented.

"Si, it is nice to ride after the rain."

"Yeah, but, it made a muddy mess to work in!" another hand replied.

"What brought you by here this mornin'?"

"Nothing particular, I was checking the creeks to see if we got much rain. I didn't have any way to measure it, so I was looking around at the places that usually catch water."

"Well, we measured about an inch and a quarter."

"That is very nice."

"Well, we gotta get back to work; thanks for stopping by."

"Adios, Seiñors."

"Yeah," came an off-hand reply.

Roberto took another round-about way back to where Daniel waited for him.

"What did it look like Roberto?"

"They are using runnin' irons, all right. I couldn't tell what brand they were changing, but it did look like they were changing a brand, not just putting on a new one."

"Nothing can happen until men from the XIT bring the sheriff, but I'll pass the word to the sheriff.

"Were any of those men John Holton?"

"No, he was not there," replied Roberto.

"Well, I'll look a while longer; maybe he'll show up."

About thirty minutes later, a man came from the house. "Quick, Roberto, come take the glasses; look."

"Si, that is John Holton." he handed the glass back to Daniel to look closer.

"I've seen him, but I have no recognition that comes to mind. At least I know what he looks like if I see him again." He paused and looked through the glasses again. "Looks like they are arguing . . . he's really letting them have it. He is starting to look around. I can't tell what he's so upset about, but he is."

"Let us go back to my home and I will fix something to eat."

"That sounds like the best thing that could happen today."

They rode back to Roberto's home, rubbed the horses down, and went inside.

Roberto warmed beans and tortillas, and poured cups of hot coffee.

"At least I got a look at Holton today. I may have had different feelings, if I had been closer to him, but as it was I will still know what he looks like. He has built a really nice home there; I guess he's dug in to stay."

After cleaning up the kitchen area, Daniel went into the bunk room to lie down. Roberto sat drinking his coffee when suddenly someone was beating on the door and shouting. "Open the door, spick! I know you're in there."

As Roberto was opening the door Holton shoved his way in, followed by another man.

Holton, a short man with a scar on his cheek and a sunburned face under a sweat stained hat, angrily yelled. "My men said you came on my place today. I want to know just what the hell you was doing over there this morning?"

"I was just riding to check the run off of the rain, and maybe visit a while, since I have no one to talk to, Señior. Your men have come to my place, so I thought I'd say howdy, as you say."

"I come to tell you that I don't want to ever see you on my place again. If I do, my men have orders to shoot you . . . you understand?" he turned and stomped out, slamming the door.

Daniel, standing by in the next room, watched Holton through the crack in the door and had been ready to burst in, if need be, to back Roberto.

"Señior, did you recognize him?"

"No, Roberto, but his name...I'm sure I heard it called after he shot me."

"Then we have made progress?"

"Maybe so, I think I will visit Charles Clement to let him know what I suspect."

"Está Bien. If you Like, I will go with you."

"Okay, they know you there. Meet me at the boarding house about sunup and I'll buy you breakfast."

"Si, I will be there."

CHAPTER 11

Daniel rode back to town. Before he went to his room, he stopped to visit with Brian Egelston, the sheriff.

As he entered he greeted the sheriff, "Howdy, Sheriff."

"Well, hello, Daniel. How are things progressing with you?"

"Still not much goin' for my memory, but I'm trying. Sheriff, I wanted to talk to you about Holton and the bunch at the BZ. You know Roberto Gonzales?"

"Yes, he comes by when he's in town."

"Well, he and I did a bit of snooping. We observed what was going on at the BZ the other day; and since we were not close enough to see exactly what was going on, Roberto went in as if on a visit. The men were cordial, they knew him. But after we were back at his place, Holton burst into his house and threatened to kill him if he ever showed up at Holton's place again. Poor Roberto didn't say anything except that he had no one to talk to, so he just gone to visit. The men were using a runnin' iron changing a brand. Roberto couldn't tell what brand was being blotched, but the only cattle within miles are the XIT cattle. I thought I would ride to headquarters to see if Charles is ready to do something. I thought I'd suggest that he take you along if he goes. Will that be all right?"

"Yes, it will. I have a couple of deputies, and I suppose you plan to go along to surprise Holton."

"I will, Sheriff. I heard a man call Holton's name after I was shot, so I'm pretty sure he was there, and he probably was the one that shot me and my family."

Daniel went to his room to get ready for supper. He washed up and changed and went downstairs to the dining room. When he was seated, Grace came and sat down with him.

"Daniel, I'm so glad you are back. Any luck?"

"Well, I nearly got Roberto Gonzales shot."

"Oh, no!" she exclaimed in a hushed voice. "Is he all right?"

"Yeah, just threatened is all."

"Who did the threatening?"

"John Holton. I know I heard his name called and someone speaking to him right after I was shot. I'm going to ride to the XIT and talk to Charles Clement. Holton may be rustling his cattle."

"Do you think he will want to do anything?"

"I certainly would think so. He may have to consult with the owners, and that will take time, so whatever he decides, I can go along with him. I just think he should know."

After he ate, Grace walked to the lobby with him.

"Be careful, Dan."

"I will, Grace."

She stretched up on her toes and kissed him.

Roberto arrived early and they sat down to a good, hearty breakfast. After they ate breakfast, and Latigo was saddled, they headed to the XIT.

The trip was uneventful and they arrived about one in the afternoon. The courtyard was deserted, so they went directly to the office and walked in.

"Daniel, back so soon?" asked Charles Clement. "Roberto Gonzales, long time no see," Charles said rising to shake their hands.

"Si, señior Clement, long time."

"What can I do for you two gentlemen?"

"Roberto and I were checking on the BZ, and they were using runnin' irons on cattle. Yours are the only ones around for miles."

Charles smiled. "You know, that would be awfully hard to do."

"Yes, but it has been done once. Even if it wasn't your brand being changed, he's on your land," said Daniel.

"Roberto, tell him what you saw."

"I rode down to talk, and they stopped what they were doing. I couldn't tell what brands they were changing, but there were lots of cattle in the pens.

Daniel spoke up. "I was at Roberto's home later when Holton beat on the door, and then he pushed his way in and threatened Roberto. Told him he would kill him if he came to the ranch again. I thought I would let you know. Sheriff Egelston said he would be willin' to go out there with you to check on what is going on if you decide to.

"The main thing I got out of watching them is when Holton busted in and shouted at Roberto, I remembered his voice and remembered I heard his name called when I was shot."

"You've convinced me I should take a look. Most of my boys are out at different places, but when they come back in a few days, I'll consider just what I want to do."

"Sounds good to me. If you need my help, I'll be available," said Daniel.

Roberto stepped closer. "You know I will be ready to help, too, señior Clement."

Daniel and Roberto headed back to Lubbock.

As they road along together, they didn't speak. Instead they just listened to the steady beat of the horses' hooves. A chaparral ran across in front of them and the horses perked their ears up and lifted their heads.

That evening, Daniel was sitting near the back of the restaurant eating his supper. Grace walked from the kitchen and went directly to Daniel's table.

"Hello, Grace."

"Hello, Dan. Did it go well today?"

"It would have gone better if you had been with me, but Roberto helped. I heard Holton's angry voice when he threatened Roberto. I'm sure he was there when my family and I were shot; I heard his name called that night by someone else who was there, too."

"I'm thinkin' Charles Clement may be ready to do something about Holton and his crew; if so, I'll be joinin' them."

"Don't you think they can handle it, Dan?"

"Yes I've no doubt they can, but I would like to be in on it, just to see Holton's face. I think I'll ride out to Roberto's and keep an eye on him and them."

"You're not going to confront them by yourself are you?" she asked.

"No, not by myself; I won't approach them unless the sheriff and Charles' bunch is there. If they suspect the XIT bunch or the sheriff is coming, they might skip, so I'll stay out of site. I may stay a day or two with Roberto."

"Just be careful, Dan."

Daniel put a few things together and loaded them on a pack horse, planning to stay out a few days and observe what was going on at the BZ bunch.

He rode toward Roberto's cabin. About half way there, he noticed smoke rising into the air. He dropped the lead rope on the pack horse and applied his spurs to Latigo. Latigo's wild horse blood leaped out to meet the challenge.

As he got closer, he could see the men throwing burning sticks on the roof of the cabin. He started firing at them, but the distance was a bit too far for his pistol. The men ran to their horses, firing back at Daniel. Latigo was running fast toward the cabin. When Daniel leaped off before the horse could stop, he ran toward the cabin. As he passed the outer door, he grabbed the canvas over the water barrel to cover his head. The roof was about all that would burn since the rest was mostly sandstone. It was an inferno, as the tar paper on the ceiling began to burn.

Running deeper into the cabin, ducking the falling debris, he saw Roberto tied to a chair, bleeding from a severe beating.

Daniel grabbed Roberto and the chair, and carried them out into the clear air. He sat the chair down, threw off the canvas tarp and took a deep breath. Roberto was unconscious.

Once Daniel had the chair separated from Roberto, he laid him on the ground away from the burning house. He took his neckerchief, ran to the water barrel and then bathed Roberto's face and neck.

When he was about ready to give up, he saw Roberto open one eye; the other one was swollen shut.

Daniel held his head up and asked him, "What happened?"

Roberto slowly looked up at Daniel. "I guess I rode too close to the BZ. Holton musta seen me. Anyway he and his men came and tied me to the chair and beat me." He passed out again.

Daniel whistled for Roberto's horse, and he came running. He saddled him, and led him to where Roberto lay; but when he got there, Roberto had died.

Daniel tied him to the saddle and headed back to town to the sheriff's office.

He tied all the horses to the hitching rack and walked through the open door.

"Hello, Daniel, what can I do for you?"

"Sheriff, Roberto is outside . . ." When Daniel paused, Sheriff Egelston said, "Well, have him come in."

"He can't, Sheriff, they've killed him!"

"Oh! Who killed him? Do you know?"

"He was alive when I got him out of his burning house, but he died while I was gittin' his horse ready to bring him to town. He said Holton and his bunch had done it. I shot at 'em, but I was too far away. I'm goin' to take him over to Cyrus' and let him get 'im ready to go into the ground. Is there anyone I need to let know, besides the XIT bunch?"

"Not that I know of, Daniel. I'm sure sorry. I'll wire the XIT and let them know what we are going to do."

"Grace will probably want to know. Charles Clement might too, since he'd worked for them so long. Roberto told me his wife died a few months ago."

"I reckon a death bed identification is good enough to go pick them up."

"Yes, sir; I say it is. Brian, some memory has returned. Not near enough, but I was sheriff in Oklahoma for a while and I sure want to go with you when you go to bring them in."

"I can certainly appreciate that, Daniel. I have two deputies; you'll make three. We can leave first thing in the morning."

CHAPTER 12

Before dawn, seven men gathered in front the sheriff's office. Daniel, Sheriff Egelston, his two deputies, Harold Evans, Jonathon Hargrave, Silas Proctor, Shorty Bates, and Sammy Estavon. They were all well-equipped. Sheriff Egelston had arranged for their breakfast.

Daniel looked at Shorty Bates and said, "Boy, you must be planning on a lot of trouble; you should be ready for anything with a Sharps fifty!"

Shorty smiled. "Cain't be too careful when you're dealing with murderers."

"True," said Daniel. "That ought to do it. Folks here in town will also know that shootin' is takin' place, 'cause they should be able to hear it!" shorty laughed.

Sheriff Egelston led out as they all headed for the BZ. As they rode along, they were quiet. Only the gentle clopping of the horses and squeaking of the saddles were heard. The horses flushed a covey of blue quail near the trail. They flew a short distance and landed to run under a chaparral bush.

Silas Proctor, mesmerized by the monotonous sounds, finally spoke up. "Damn shame what they did to Roberto. We ought to hang 'em on the spot."

Sheriff Egelston responded, "Now none of that; they'll get their day in court. Thing is, we got a witness to two murders that took place before Roberto."

Sammy Estavon said, "We do? Who would that be?"

"This man right here riding beside me."

Sammy's eyes got big as he looked at Daniel. "I thought he couldn't remember nothin' least that's what I heard."

"Well, you heard right, but since then he has been remembering a lot of things; and one was he heard Holton's name called as the shooter of his wife and his son.

"Kinda looks like Holton is goin' to have a lot of trouble getting out of this one," said Sammy.

The others were getting ahead of the sheriff, so he spurred his horse and caught up with Harold Evans.

It was hot, shadows were getting smaller as noon approached and the sun was moving overhead. Occasionally, the trail became fine dust and swirled up as high as the riders. A couple of grasshoppers buzzed up and flew away. In the hot sun, the steady sound of the hoof beats caused the men to fight to stay awake.

Daniel wiped his brow, and then the inside band of his hat with his handkerchief. "I reckon we should have started last night; this heat makes me sleepy."

Sheriff Egelston nodded. "We'll be there pretty quick. It's a lot shorter this way, than going to Roberto's house.

Soon the house of John Holton came into sight. "We'll ride right on up to his porch," said Sheriff Egelston.

Holton saw them coming, took up his coffee and walked out onto the porch. As they go closer, he stepped off the porch and walked to meet them. "Well, hello, Sheriff; what brings you way off out here? I haven't been in to town lately. Has they been a robbery or somethin'?"

Sheriff Egelston stepped down and walked toward Holton, closely watching the two other men who had come out of the house. "John, you better come along with me. Your hired hands, too."

"What fer Sheriff? You need some help with somethin'?"

"No, John. It's because of what you and your hands done to Roberto."

"Roberto? What about Roberto?"

"Don't try to play me, John; you know very well what happened."

One of the men on the porch, knowing someone had seen them throwing fire on Roberto's house because he had shot at them, started to go for his gun, when a tremendous explosion sounded. Shorty, sitting near Daniel's right side, had fired his Sharps 50 while Sammy close on Daniel's left, shot his Winchester 45 at the same time. The concussion of big guns came from both sides of Daniel. Latigo, startled by the very loud noise of both guns, gave a couple of pretty hardy jumps; and, unprepared, Daniel hit the ground.

Both of Holton's men were dead, Daniel was covered with dust, and Holton was fighting with the Sheriff.

Quickly, Harold Evans hit Holton with his rifle butt, and the fight was over.

Since Daniel was on the ground anyway, he moved to the corral and saddled a horse for John Holton.

As Holton was coming around, he said, "Sheriff, you had no right bustin' in here and killing two of my men and roustin' me. They must'a done old Roberto in on their own!

"I'm also arresting you for the murder of Jennifer and Adam Fleming, and the attempted murder of Daniel Fleming."

"What you mean . . . attempted murder?"

As Daniel walked up leading the horse for Holton to use, he said, "Yes, attempted murder of me!"

Holton's eyes got bigger and his mouth dropped open as he stared at Daniel, and then he said, "But . . . you was shot twice. I, ah, I mean . . ."

The Sheriff interrupted his stammering. "Enough said. Get him on his horse."

Shorty Proctor said, "Ain't we gonna hang him here Sheriff?"

Sammy smiled real big and said, "Can't do that, Shorty. He'll get his day in court, and then we'll hang him!

Daniel climbed back on Latigo, shook his head and smiled, saying, "Shorty . . . Sammy, I want'a thank you two."

"Shorty looked at him and asked, "What fer, Dan'l?"

Sammy chimed in. "Yeah, what fer?"

"Well, fellers, I'm sure you didn't notice, but when you two fired those cannons, and Latigo tossed me . . . that entire episode brought my memory back, and Sheriff, I was tempted to shoot Holton right here and now!"

Brian blinked. "Well, I'm glad you didn't, Daniel. After all you've been through; I would hate to have to arrest you. You say you remember everything?"

"Everything!"

They placed John Holton on his horse, tied him to his saddle, and headed back to town.

"Shorty, I think we need a beer when we get back," commented Sammy.

"Amen to that," Shorty agreed.

Daniel said, "And I'm payin'!"

As they rode back, the excitement had died away. Shorty, riding next to Daniel, noticed his head hanging low and tears staining his cheek, but wouldn't mention it. He rode close to Daniel, so no one else would see. They pulled up in front of the Jail and stepped down by the horse watering trough. Shorty said, "I don't know about you, but I'm gonna wash some of this dirt off my face."

Daniel watched a minute, and then agreed. "That's a good idea," and took his hat off and generously washed.

After they had Holton locked up, they went to the saloon to unwind.

"Well, Dan'l, now you got your memory back, what did you do before? asked Sammy.

"I did a lot of ranchin', cowboyin', and farmin', and I was sheriff in Oklahoma after bein' a deputy for years. I ran across Charles Clement up in Colorado, and he asked me to take over one of the XIT farms. . . . I never made it to that farm."

Sheriff Egelston set his empty bottle down on the table. "Daniel I can use a permanent deputy; Harold has other jobs he has to do and can't be available always, so if that suits you, I can use you both. I'd be glad to have you."

"I think that is exactly what I want to do. Can you give me a few days? I just need some time alone."

"Sure, no problem just come around when you're ready."

"Oh, Brian, would you mind sending another wire to Charles Clement to let him know that Holton has been taken care of?"

"Sure thing, Daniel; be glad to."

From there, Daniel went to the cemetery on the edge of town. As he stood by Jennifer and Adam's graves, he said, "It took a while, but now I can feel the hole left in my heart without you. I don't know if I said it and it may be too late to say it now, but I loved you both very much, and I will miss you for the rest of my life."

It was getting late, near time for supper, so, Daniel headed for the boarding house to wash up and eat. He moved to the table where he liked to sit, with his back to the wall.

As soon as Grace saw him; she moved to his table and sat down.

"Evening Daniel, I was so sorry to hear about Roberto. Did things go well today?"

"Better than I can explain. We were able to get Holton and his bunch; however, Holton is the only one alive."

"I'm glad, Daniel, for your sake."

"Grace, I'm gonna take a few days and ride around. While I was at the Holton place, I had an experience that brought my memory back, full bore. I can remember everything."

"Oh, Daniel, I'm so glad for you. I think it will be good for you to get away for a while."

"I would like you to be with me, but . . .

"Take all the time you need. I'll wait."

He looked at Grace, then down at the table. "Brian says he will take me on as full time deputy."

"I knew you had been in law enforcement before, so that should be a good fit."

"Yeah, besides, I'm libel to run out of money before long."

He stood up to leave. Grace came around the table. As she did, she whispered, "A little something to take with you."

She caught his arms, stretched up, and kissed him.

"Thank you, Grace. I won't stay away too long." She smiled as he moved toward the door.

Grace called, "Dan, do you want Georgia to load you up?"

"I guess I had better. She knows what I like; two or three days will be enough. I can handle a lot of jerky. Thanks for reminding me."

CHAPTER 13

Daniel was up early and went to the livery. Chester was up working already. Daniel asked, with a chuckle, "Do you live here, Chester?"

"In a way, if I'm here early I feel like I do, but if I'm still at home when folks come by, that means they fix things themselves."

"I guess you got plenty of feed in all my horses."

"I shore do. They eat for five!"

"Put it on my bill. I got a job now, but I'll be out for a few days."

"Will do," answered Chester.

As he finished putting the pack on his Bay, he stroked the horse's neck. "And now I know that you're Sunsine, Adam's horse." He turned and rubbed the neck of the roan and said, "And I know you are Dolly, Jennifer's horse." He then gave Latigo's cinch another pull. "Well, Latigo, I'm sorry I didn't know you there for a while, but I'm back now and I hope you'll help me figure things out."

He mounted and headed south. Soon the sun peaked over the horizon putting pink on the small puffy white clouds, and shooting gold rays into the sky. He could see for miles across the vast openness to buttes spotted randomly on the Llano Estacato. The breeze the sun generated as it pushed above the horizon of the expanse of land caused the grass to wave.

"Boy, Latigo. It's good to be riding, knowing who I am, and who you are." He turned in the saddle toward his pack horse. "And you, too, Sunshine." Ears moved, but Daniel doubted they understood.

Daniel pulled up. "You know, I just think I'll change directions and head north. I think I'd like to talk to Charles Clement again. Besides, I sure like the vittles they hand out. I need to time my arrival just right. It's a long way there. I hope I don't wear you out." He saw another flick of the ears in acknowledgement.

Daniel rode to the breaks north of Lubbock, rode down into a wash where he found a large hangover cut into the banks by water over the years.

When he spotted a buffalo wallow with water he let the horses drink. He checked the height of the sun, and then decided to make camp, because he didn't know how far it would be to another source of water.

He removed the saddle and the pack from the horses and turned them loose; he knew a whistle would bring both. The grass was good all along the higher end of the wash, so he knew they would stay close.

Next day, he continued to circle around Lubbock, and headed to Plainview and on up toward that new town, Dalhart.

About ten days later, he arrived at the headquarters of the XIT, tied his horses loosened the cinches and stepped up on the porch, then entered. Charles was sitting behind what he called a desk.

"Well, well, our good friend Daniel Fleming. Good to see you . . . come in; sit down and tell me what you've been doing.

"Sheriff Egelston wired that y'all were headed to the Holton place . . . how'd that turn out?"

Daniel sat down in the chair in front of the desk. "Well, I guess for you, very good. Holton is in custody, his hands killed off, and I got my memory back. I apologize again for not making it and not being able to let you know about what was going on."

"You got your memory back? That's great! It must have been rough on you not knowing who you were."

"It was, but now I'm ready to start a new life. My old one was a beautiful thing, until Holton came into it!"

"I can understand; at least I can imagine."

"Oh, yes. I needed to let you know that Roberto was killed by Holton and his crew, and they burned his house . . . the roof mostly."

Charles shook his head sadly. "That's a darn shame . . . he was a good man."

"Yes, he was. He helped me watch the Holton bunch, until I recognized what he had to do with our family shooting. I'm just out riding, trying to decide what to do. Sheriff Egelston has offered me a deputy job. I'm used to that kinda work, so all's good I guess."

"Stay for supper, and then stay in the bunkhouse tonight. That away you can get a fresh start in the morning. But before you go, tell me about the land and all that Holton cut for what he was calling 'his place'."

"I was hopin' you would ask me to chow down; I been eatin' jerky for days. The land was holding the grass well. There has been some rain, enough to keep the grazing up and the cattle fat. He had built corrals, a real nice house, and a small bunkhouse that will sleep about eight."

"Well, do me a favor. Move into it and keep it up for me. If you find any cattle from the XIT, keep them in shape; and when you sell them, use the money as a salary."

"That's mighty generous of you, Charles."

"Not really, Daniel. You've saved me a great deal of trouble; besides, my men work in that area a lot and you can take care of them. Too, I wouldn't want a nice house to go to waste. Now, let's go eat."

Daniel was up with the rest of the men, washed up and headed for the kitchen. He did the small talk about the condition of cattle here, how much rain had they gotten and other generalities; and then he got on his way.

It had been a while since they had had rain in the area, and the ground was dry. Little puffs of dust flipped up from beneath the horse's hooves.

"Latigo, let's go home. I've done enough ride-about. I'd like to see a certain beautiful lady before long." The usual ear flipping indicated Latigo heard . . . and probably understood.

CHAPTER 14

Daniel arrived in Lubbock late in the evening, took care of his horses, and then headed to the boarding house. He stepped up on the porch with intentions of washing up and going to bed. He noticed the big door was left open to let the cool evening breeze pass through the room. As he entered the big door and stepped on the landing of the stairs, Grace rushed out of her room and called his name.

Hearing her voice, he turned and walked directly to her, put his arms around her and kissed her.

She smiled and said, "I missed that,"

He continued to hold her. "I may never let you go."

"That will be fine with me."

"I have a lot to tell you, but it can wait until tomorrow."

"The food is still warm, let's go to the kitchen and I'll get you a plate."

"I'd really appreciate that, even though I ate so much at the XIT I didn't think I'd ever have to eat again. I rode hard today just to get back. I think I stopped only once to let ole Latigo and Sunshine have water, and rest a little. We're all tired, but they were eating when I left."

She smiled. "Ah, so it's Sunshine, is it?"

"Yeah, that was Adam's horse. Is there more coffee?"

She headed to the kitchen. "It'll only take a minute. The fresh pot of coffee is still on the stove. Some of the guests like to come down late for a cup, so I make a fresh one before I retire for the night. If you will get the coffee, I'll get your food."

He went to the stove, poured a cup and sat back down.

Soon Grace had prepared bacon and eggs with a couple of buttered biscuits left from the evening meal.

"I fixed you breakfast. I thought that would be better than something warmed over."

"I thought I smelled bacon. Grace this is just right after a hard day."

"Was your trip a good one?"

"Yes it was. I was going to wait until tomorrow, but this seems the right time. Charles Clement wrote a permission note for me to occupy the place that Holton built. The cattle there that belonged to the XIT can be used for breeding and to pay a salary. The only stipulation is that if he sends cowboys to work that area, they are to stay there while they work. The ranch will keep it supplied for when we have men come.

I described what all was on the place, and when he heard that it had a bunkhouse, he came up with that idea."

She sat down across from him, and as she did she asked, "So you can live there? Wait, what? For we . . . **we** have men there? We who?"

"I had hoped that **we** can live there. You and me."

"Daniel Fleming, are you purposing to me?"

"Yes, I am, Grace, if you'll have me."

"Oh, Dan, that will make me *so* happy"

He placed a ring on her finger. "I hope you don't mind, Grace. This ring was in my saddlebags. It was Jennifer's; it's all I have."

"I don't mind, Dan. I'm honored to wear it. It can serve as both an engagement and a wedding ring. I know you loved the heart it bound before, and will love the heart that it binds to you now."

After a moment of silence, he said, "I thought we could ride out, when you can get loose, to look it over to see what is needed to make it our home."

"I can get loose right away to do that. Dan, are you sure you want to do this? Have you really thought about it long enough?"

"I've never wanted to do anything as much as I want to do this! And yes I've thought of nothing else."

"You've ridden an awful lot lately, but will tomorrow be too soon?" she asked.

"Are you kidding? I was born to ride; besides I didn't get a look at the place when I was there. Outside, it looked like it would make a good home with a little work."

"I really hope that it is not too soon for you; I'm just anxious," she admitted.

"Okay, it's settled then; I need another cup of coffee!"

"Oh, you!" She stood up. "You can get it yourself. I'm going to bed. I have a hard day coming tomorrow. Good night." She bustled off leaving him sitting alone.

"I guess that's my signal to go to bed, too."

CHAPTER 15

Next morning, Grace and Georgia were stirring around the kitchen preparing breakfast. Grace had explained why she would be out today.

When she finished telling her, Georgia said, "Uh Huh, I done tolls you he had a mighty crush on you. I's shore glad you listened, honey; he'll do all right by you," she let out a hearty laugh before saying, "I shore is right."

Grace smiled at her and said, "If you're through analyzing my love life, we will need food for a few days. I don't know how many, but we'll manage."

Georgia laughed. "Uh huh, y'all can just live on love when de food runs out." She turned away laughing.

"I'll serve until Betty Jane gets here."

"And then you be gone. Honey, I envy you. When I got married first time, we live in a box car," confided Georgia.

Daniel got all three horses ready, two saddled and one ready to take on the pack.

"Chester, I imagine they've eaten enough to last a few days, haven't they?"

"Yep, and that grass up north got a good rain, according to Will James. He was up that way the other day; said the grass was knee high to his horse, so it ought to satisfy them with good grazin'."

He led the horses up to the boarding house, tied them at the hitching posts, and went inside.

"Are you about ready to go, Grace?"

"As soon as Betty Jane gets here."

"Georgia, you goin' with us? It could be fun."

"Nawsir, Mista Fleming; Ia's needed here, I reckons."

"Well, I'll miss you."

"You jus' miss da cookin'; I knows you. Sides you taken my hep away, leave me pracoly to myself."

"I'll make it up to you, Georgia."

"I gonna holds you to dat."

Daniel stepped close to her and gave her a peck on the cheek.

"You cain't make up that easy, now . . . you two go on out o' here."

Grace whispered to Georgia. "Thank you; see you soon."

They went outside and Daniel tightened the cinches. "Grace, I want you to meet Dolly."

"Well, hello Dolly. This was Jennifer's, I guess."

"Yep; she's gentle too, if you ever want to ride when I'm gone with Latigo and Sunshine."

"She's pretty."

"Yeah; a Roan is a pretty horse. I made up a sugan for you; we'll have to camp some. Also, we don't have any idea what shape the house is in."

"That's fine, Dan. I like sleeping outside."

"The weather is good right now; very pleasant for sleeping."

They rode for quite a while, but they found no water for the horses. "The canteens will have to do to moisten the horse's mouths. We should run across a little water before our canteens run out. We'll ride down in the draw. Chester said he heard they had rain recently, so we might find a trickle down in here. They eased down in the draw and rode until Grace noticed a dark streak on the yellow sandstone.

"Look, Dan. Isn't that dark streak there on the side caused by water?"

"I believe you're right." He dismounted and dug at the source of the streak, and a large seep started to run down the rock. When it did, Daniel took his canteen and caught the water as it trickled from the rock.

"I'll let it puddle up so the horses can drink"

"I filled our canteen, so we can make it to the ranch okay. I was sure I saw buffalo wallows on this trail. Cattle make trails all the time. I guess this isn't the one I traveled last time."

They arrived at the ranch well before dark.

Grace surveyed the entire scene then commented. "Oh, Dan, it will fix up nice, won't it?"

"I believe it will. It might take time to get what we need up here, but a good wagon can carry a lot of stuff."

They went inside. "Dan, it really looks nice, and it looks as if it's been taken care of."

"Grace, honey?" She whirled around and stared at him.

"What?" he asked feeling perplexed.

"That's the first time you've called me 'Honey'."

He smiled at her. "It probably won't be the last time, because you are that sweet."

She turned away from him, because she knew she was blushing.

He walked up behind her and put his arms around her. She turned to face him. "Grace, I've come for some honey. He pulled her close and kissed her.

"That will have to last you a while; we've got a lot to check out, Daniel."

"Okay, you're the doctor. I'll go check the water situation."

He spun around and went out the door to the screened-in back porch. There he found a pump and gave it a push or two, but nothing came forth. He lifted the wooden lid, looked in, and mumbled, "I'm not going to waste our canteen water to prime that pump." He let the lid back down, and went outside, searching a bit. Then he came back in, lifted the lid again, and dropped a small rock into the well and listened. It took a few seconds for it to reach the water with a splash. "Well, we have water anyway," he muttered.

He came back inside and found Grace checking everything out. "We have water anyway."

"I know! There's a pump at the kitchen sink and it works well," she exclaimed gleefully.

"They must have put that in after the one on the porch," surmised Daniel. He tried the one in the kitchen. "No wonder! This is not a pump, it's a bucket chain. Little buckets dip up the water from the well and they then dump the water into the spout when it gets to the top."

"I don't care how it gets to the sink. I'm just glad it does," she declared.

"I'll go take care of the horses and get us something to eat."

"Leave the door open when you go out, please. There was a great breeze that came through when you came in."

Daniel took care of the horses and brought supplies into the house. The saddles, he put in the barn. He then went out back to look at the cattle that were grazing nearby. *They looked good and most are wearing the XIT brand. We should have a lot of stock soon.*

Back inside, he approached Grace. "We have some good looking cattle. I gotta say Holton had a good eye when he stole cattle. There are a few we will have to return to the owners. Some may be hard to locate, because the brands have been changed. There's a good tank out there and it's full of water. I guess the last rain was a good one."

"Most everything we need to make this our home is already here, so it won't take us long," she observed. "But we have to get rid of a bunch of clothes and stuff that was Holton's."

They both sat down on the plump sofa.

"You know, it takes quite a while to get to Lubbock. You can't ride that far every day."

She thought a moment. "I can ride in on Friday, work the weekend and come back for a while during the week until we can make some money with the cattle."

"I don't want you to ride that trail alone. I'd rather you, or both of us, stay in town and kinda visit here every once in a while, 'till we get it going like we want to. Besides, I have a little money left."

"I have some savings, too, and I might just give the place to Georgia and let her give me a little of the profit . . . when it makes some, that is."

"We'll make it fine," he said and leaned toward her for another kiss. I think we've hit it lucky...not a tremendous amount of work to do.

"I'll come back in a day or two and take care of the things that need work. You need to think about what needs to be done for the wedding."

"Oh, I forgot about that," she said laughingly.

"You *forgot* about that?"

"No, I didn't, silly; but it was fun watching your face. Let's eat."

Daniel got up and walked into the kitchen. Through the window he could see the road leading to the place, and a couple of riders were coming up the road. They moved slowly, observing the layout of the ranch. Daniel said, "Grace, get in the closet and if you can, lock it."

"What's going on, Dan?"

"Two riders are coming up the road. I can't tell if they are alone. Go!"

She headed to the closet, and he went out on the porch.

"Howdy, fellers," he greeted them.
"Kinda hot out, isn't it."

"It sure is."

Daniel handed a canteen to one of the men and asked, "Been ridin' far?

"Purdy far, today, we are looking for a man named Holton. He wrote to hire us to take care of some problems he was havin'."

"He's not here anymore. You can check on him in Lubbock."

"We come a long way; got a place we can spend the night?"

"You're welcome to spend the night in the barn, if that's okay. The last owner didn't leave me the key to the bunk house and I don't want to bust up a good door; they are hard to come by way out here. I just hadn't had a chance to work on it yet."

"Sure, that suits us."

"Just turn your horses in to the corral with the others. There's a mite of corn in there; I expect they'll need that."

"They can shore use it," said one of the men.

"I'll bring you a bucket of water. There are some small pieces of wood to start you a fire out there."

"Many thanks," they rode around to the barn and stepped down, took care of their horses, stripped their saddles, and one said, "I reckon we'll sleep outside; it'll be cooler."

"Well, whatever you want. I'd check it out, though. The barn is built out of thick sandstone so it may be cooler inside."

"We'll check it out, thanks."

Daniel went inside and spoke to Grace through the door. "Grace, you can come out now, but watch and move quickly by any window, and don't go outside."

"What is it, Dan?"

"They were looking for Holton; said he hired them. Just don't let them see you. I know their kind. It wouldn't be safe. I'll make sure they leave tomorrow. They just might know Holton is in jail."

Daniel and Grace worked with things inside the house and ate their supper. "Grace, I know you're tired, so go on to bed; I'll sleep on the couch as we planned. That way I can keep an eye on things. I'll help you strip the bed to put your sugan on it."

"Thanks, Dan, Are we going to have trouble living here?"

"No, it's just things that were arranged before we got Holton that could be a problem. I told them that Holton was in Lubbock. I'll try to get them to move on without telling them he's in jail."

He helped her with her make-shift bed, kissed her goodnight, and made his bed on the couch.

About three in the morning, Daniel was awakened by the squeak in the back door that he had planned to fix. *I didn't lock that door. It's a good thing I didn't fix the squeak. Someone's coming in,* he thought, as he sat up, gun ready to meet the intruder.

When the man moved across the room he passed in front of a window, enabling Daniel to see his silhouette. "Hold it right there."

As he spoke a flaming blaze and blast came from the shadow. Daniel felt the tug on his sleeve and the jolt of the bullet hitting him. Instinctively he fired rounds in several directions to make sure of a hit. He heard the man hit the floor. Then he heard the back door squeak again, and he braced himself to watch for the other man to cross in front of the window. He heard the man ask, "Did you get him Bob?"

Daniel fired as soon as he saw the man cross in front of the window. He then reached over and lifted the chimney of the lamp and struck a match. As he did, he watched in the direction of the men, so he wouldn't be taken by surprise, and then he put the match to the wick and replaced the chimney. A warm yellow glow filled the room.

Grace opened the door just a crack and peeked out. When she saw Daniel sitting on the couch, she asked, "Is it over?"

"Yes, it's over, but you better have a look at this arm."

It was then she saw the blood. "Dan, you're hit! Let me see." She ran to him and started unbuttoning his shirt.

"You're not going to take advantage of me are you, Grace?"

"Aw, Dan, this is not time for foolin . . . "

Before she could finish he pulled her down on the couch and began kissing her. She didn't resist, but did pull back saying, "Let me see that wound; you may bleed to death!"

"If I do it in your arms, I'll be the happiest man alive . . . or dead."

"Dan, how can you joke at a time like this? You may be seriously hurt."

"That's the effect you have on me."

"What? That I'm a joke to you?"

"No. That you make me happy no matter how bad I hurt."

She breathed a sigh of relief. "This is just a scratch; it will probably be all right by morning."

Dan cocked his head. "Just in case, I'll put a little kerosene on it after a while."

"You're going to put that stinky stuff on your wound?"

"Yes, ma'am; it helps the healing. I use it all the time."

"Well, when we are married, don't put any on unless you're working outside, and certainly not before bedtime!"

"Oh, honey, I promise. Now I'd best get these two fellers in the ground, before they . . ."

She cut him off "Don't say it . . . just go do it."

"I might need your help; after all, I'm wounded."

She threw his shirt at him.

He dug a big grave, pulled the men out and covered them. Then he laid sandstone slabs left over from building the barn and house on top to prevent varmints from disturbing them.

When he had the grave completed, he went back into the house. Grace was cleaning the floor. He pumped water and splashed it on the floor, then helped her finish.

"Dan, I think we've done about all we can do this trip. Next time we'll bring the wagon and move in."

"That sounds like a plan."

When they arrived back in Lubbock, Grace went to the boarding house and Daniel went to the sheriff's office.

"Sheriff, I had a little trouble up at the place."

"Oh . . . what kind of trouble?"

"Two men showed up; said Holton hired them. In the night they came into the house. One shot me, and then I shot them both."

"I see; was one tall with a thin mustache and the other one a little heavy with a green handkerchief?"

"Yeah, how'd you know?"

"They came in here, wanting to see Holton."

"I guess you let them in."

"I did, but I'll not let anyone else see him 'till he's moved to the State prison."

"Thanks, Brian."

He led Latigo across the street and tossed the reins over the hitch rack, went in and walked into the kitchen. "Is dinner ready, yet?" Georgia was the only one in there.

"Yesser, it sure is. Now you go sits down.

"Miss Sewell is cleaning up after that ride. She be here in a minute."

"Thank you, Georgia. I missed your cookin' while I was gone."

"What's you mean? I fixed you a lot a cookin' ta take."

"I mean hot off the stove cookin'. The kind you sit back, loosen your belt and say, ahhhh over."

Grace came in about that time. Daniel stood, pulled out a chair, and she sat down.

"My." He paused as if looking her over. "Beautiful lady, do you live around here? I don't believe I've seen such beauty around here before."

"I just came in on the stage from Plainview," she said in a sappy Southern drawl while batting her eyelashes at him.

Georgia walked up with their plates and rolled her eyes at them. "You two beats all I evah seen; lawdy, lawdy." She turned and walked back to the kitchen shaking her head and cackling with laughter.

"Grace, you can't give this place to her. We're gonna take her with us!"

"I'd like that, Dan, but we will need the income for a while, and someone who knows the business has to be here, and she's the best."

"Tell me about it," he groaned. "Grace, I guess it's a bath for me now."

"I had mine while you were at the sheriff's office."

CHAPTER 16

Three men rode into town and stopped in front of the jail and tied their horses. Two walked in. Brian Egelston stood up behind his desk and asked, "Can I help you fellers?"

"We came to visit our Uncle, John Holton," said the taller of the two. "We been traveling for six days. Thought we'd come visit him first, then go on up to our aunt's house in Plainview."

"Well, gentlemen, I'm sorry but that's not possible. You see he's . . ." Brian, thinking quickly, continued, "...a *certified prisoner*, and no one is allowed to visit with him until he is moved to a state facility."

Brian had no idea the third man gone around to the back of the jail cells.

Inside one cell, John Holton heard a low whisper from outside his cell window call to him. He stood on his cot and looked through the bars. "Jesse, I thought you guys were never goin' to get here."

"Yeah, Flip and Johnson are in talkin' to the sheriff. He won't let us in. I heard him say you're a specified prisoner...or something like that. I don't know what that means, but he said they can't come in."

Holton whispered, "Get some paper and a pencil. I'll give you the name of the one I want taken care of, and I'll write a note for the bank to give you your money."

"All right; be back in a little while."

As the two men exited the office, the third man joined them. He spoke quietly. "I talked to Holton. He wants some paper and a pencil to write the name of the man we're here to take care of, and he said he'll write a note to the bank so they'll give us our money."

"Good. Flip, you got any paper?"

"Naw; I got a stub of a pencil, though."

"Well, go across the street and get some from that store."

"When you get it, take it to Holton so he can write the information down. We won't all hang out behind the jail. Someone might get suspicious. When you get the note from him, we'll meet you in the saloon. I want to go to the bank after we get that note, so's we'll have the money in hand and can leave right away."

Flip ran over to the mercantile. The only paper he could find was a Big Chief tablet. He grabbed it, paid for it, and hurried out the door. The clerk walked out after him and shook his head, wondering why a guy like that would want to buy a tablet in such a hurry.

He watched the man until he disappeared behind the jail, and then he wondered, *why would a man run behind the jail with a Big Chief tablet?* Puzzled, he walked back inside his store.

Holton wrote the note to the bank, and then on another piece of paper he wrote, *Daniel Fleming.* "This man helps the sheriff, so he'll be easy to identify. If you hang around the saloon, somebody will call his name," he whispered through the cell bars.

Flip nodded and took the paper to Johnson, who headed toward the bank. Turning the corner, he saw the bank was closed. Irritated, he wheeled around and headed back to the saloon, where he met the other two sitting at a table near the rear wall.

"The bank was closed, so we can't get out money 'til tomorrow," he grumbled. We can't take out this Fleming guy first, because we gotta be ready to get out of town real quick." What they didn't know, but would find out later, was that Daniel had asked the banker to freeze Holton's account, so they couldn't get the money anyway.

Daniel looked for Grace, but she had left the boarding house, so he checked outside. As he stepped out on the street, he saw a flash of the blue dress he knew she was wearing. She was heading into the mercantile, so he followed her.

"Grace, we need to talk. I'll meet you back at home in thirty minutes if that's okay."

"Why, of course, Daniel. I'll be through here in a few minutes."

He started to leave when Jacob called his name.

"Daniel, I don't know if there is anything to it, but some fellow came in here a while ago and purchased a Big Chief tablet, and then walked behind the jail."

"Huh, that's a bit odd. Thanks, Jacob. I'll check it out."

Daniel walked over to corner of the lane running behind the jail, took his hat off, and peeked around the edge of the building. He looked both ways down the lane behind the jail, but no one was there.

Half out loud he mumbled, "No one there now, but he could have talked to Holton through the cell window," he said surveying the area further.

He returned to the mercantile store, stepped up on the porch and walked in. Grace had finished her business and left.

"Jacob, what'd this feller look like?"

"Well, let's see," he said scratching his head. "He was thin, bent over at the shoulders, a little mustache and scrubby goatee. His hat was torn at the brim. I thought maybe I would be able to sell him a hat when he took the tablet, but that was all he wanted."

"Thank you, Jacob; I'll watch for him. I'm pretty sure he was getting it for Holton's use."

"Ya think? What fer, ya 'spose?"

"No telling, Jacob. Thanks again."

Daniel and Grace went back to the boarding house to talk.

"Grace, honey, I've got to look for a feller down at the saloon, but I'll be right back. I think something is going on with Holton."

"I'll be here," she called out "I like it when you call me honey, honey," she said smiling mischievously.

He smiled back at her and went out into the street toward the saloon. Stepping onto the walk he looked over the swinging doors and spotted the man described by Jacob sitting with two others near the back of the saloon. He walked in and stood by some of the men at the bar. Facing the bar, he just listened a while.

In a low voice, the mousey looking man asked, "What'd he write on the paper? I can't read."

The man next to him quietly said, "Just a name...Daniel Fleming."

"That the one we're sup----?"

"Shut up, you idiot!"

"Okay, okay, I just wanted to . . ."

"Enough!" he hissed. Go on down and saddle the horses. Keep your mouth shut!" Grumbling under his breath, the man did as he was told.

The one doing all the talking was the one called Jesse. He motioned for the bartender to come close. "Do you know a man named Daniel Fleming?"

"Shore do; he helps the Sheriff."

"Yeah, that's the one."

"Do you need to talk to him?" the bartender asked.

"Well, yes and no."

"Well, when you decide, he's the tall fellow standing at the end of the bar." He chuckled and walked away.

Daniel turned to him and said, "Howdy; can I help you? I'm Daniel Fleming."

Jesse froze saying nothing; then managed to force out words against his fear. "Uh, yeah. How--howdy! I heard you worked with the sheriff. I know what he looks like and I thought I'd get acquainted with ya so I'd know what both of you looked like in case I needed your help. Glad to meet you, ah, Mister, er, Daniel."

The man finished his drink and left. Daniel noticed he seemed very nervous.

The bartender stepped back to Daniel. "What was that all about, Daniel?"

"I have an idea he's cookin' somethin' up with Holton, but I don't know what . . . yet."

Daniel left the saloon and headed back to talk to Grace.

"What did you want to talk about, Daniel?"

"I've been arguing with myself, and have decided I need to go to the Three Rivers reservation in Oklahoma to talk to Jennifer's mother, Laughing Dove, and the agent and his wife she grew up with. Laughing Dove stayed close to Jennifer even though she was raised and educated by the Severs. They would need to know, so they can help Laughing Dove morn. It's a complicated affair for those of us who don't know the heart and spirit of the Indians."

"I know what you mean, Dan. Yes, it needs to be done. Be careful and hurry back. I'll have Georgia fix you a travel larder."

"Thank you for understanding, Grace. I will hurry back."

He loaded a pack to put on the horse in the morning, and rubbed both Latigo and Sunshine down, fed them grain and talked to them. "I'll see you in the morning; we've a long trip ahead."

Before grey came to the sky, Daniel was bound for Muskogee, Oklahoma. It was a cool morning, and quiet except for the doves calling for mates.

He had not traveled more than five miles when he saw a flash that came from behind a rock a few hundred yards ahead.

"Latigo, did you see that?" Latigo flicked his ears. "Sun on a gun barrel. Looks like whoever it is in an amateur. Well, I guess we will have to take care of it. You keep on movin'; Sunshine will follow you."

He stepped off Latigo's right side without stopping and moved off to the right into the rocks. He went up and across them hurriedly and moved forward. He positioned himself so that the sun was at his back and in the eyes of those waiting for him to ride by. Latigo continued to walk slowly down the road with Sunshine following behind paying no attention that Daniel was no longer with them. The saddle still squeaked and the hoof sounds had not changed since Daniel stepped off. When the horses were even with their hiding place, three men stepped out into the trail, guns drawn. Latigo and Sunshine stopped.

They were astonished to learn Daniel was not on his horse. Bewildered, they looked at each other and back at the horses.

Daniel stepped from behind the rocks above them and spoke quietly. "Are you lookin' for me?"

The three turned and began shooting. Daniel ducked behind the rocks and returned fire. They were in the open. They didn't stand a chance.

When the smoke cleared, Daniel dropped down to the trail and examined each man. He found one still alive.

"Holton sent you to your death. I'm very sorry, but you chose the route you took. I'm also sorry because whatever he promised to pay you, he did not have; so, this entire episode could have been avoided."

The man opened his eyes and looked straight into Daniel's. "I would not be here if the bank had been open." His eyes closed and he was gone.

It's a shame how little preparation people make in life, Daniel thought.

He dragged each man into a small ravine and pushed the loose dirt over them and placed some rocks on top to discourage varmints and vultures.

When he a had finished, he stood, checked the sun, wiped the sweat from inside his hat, and decided he had at least three more hours before he would stop for the night.

That evening after he finished eating, he sat by his fire sipping coffee and watching a lizard attempting to carry a bug almost too big for him. He mused, "Feller, you've got a lot of work to do, but at least you are close to home. Here I am with four hundred miles to go. If all goes well, I should make it in less than a month."

He stomped out his small fire and placed his coffee pot beside it to be warmed in the morning.

Next morning as he saddled Latigo and placed the pack on Sunshine, he commented, "Sorry that I have very little grain right now, but I will have some for you tonight.

The farther north he rode, the grass grew greener and was in good shape, high enough for Latigo and Sunshine to grab mouthfuls and eat as they went along.

Soon he was surprised when he rode up on the south rim of the Palo Duro Canyon.

"Great day!" he spoke out loud, "So this is the big canyon; I've heard about it, but this is the first time I've seen it. Latigo, this may be a challenge." He turned east and rode along the edge of the canyon looking for a way to ride across. As he rode along, he soon came to a faint Indian trail where Comanche had entered the canyon years ago. Some of the switch-backs had places that rain had washed out, but Daniel was able to ride to the bottom.

He was also surprised to see a few buffalo as he rode across. "Buffalo! I thought they were all gone, yet here they are. Ranch buffalo. It saddens me to know that millions of these great animals once roamed this land and now most are gone. I'll have to bring Grace here; it is truly beautiful."

Late one day as he rode through the trees along a creek, he caught the faint smell of smoke. Thinking it was from a campfire; he became more alert and started to search for the source, thinking he might have someone to join up with. Soon, he saw through the trees the flicker of the flames of a fire that was far too large for just cooking.

He cautiously approached, and then he hailed the camp. "Hellooo the camp, can I come in?"

The response surprised him. A small voice of a young boy answered, "Come on in."

Daniel approached and to his surprise a boy of ten or so was poking at the fire with a long stick. He could tell the boy had been crying. There were tear trails down through the dust that had gathered on his cheeks.

Daniel asked, "Mind if I get down and join you?"

Sadly, the boy replied, "No, sir, but I got no supplies."

"Have you eaten anything?"

"No, sir, I ain't et; I got nothin' to eat."

Daniel went back to Sunshine and took his water bucket from the strings tying it to the pack and handed it to the boy. "Take this canvas bucket and get some water from the creek. Dip lightly so's to not get a lot of mud. I'll put together something for us to eat."

The boy took the bucket and headed to the creek. When he returned, Daniel was setting a skillet full of bacon on the fire.

The boy's eyes widened when he saw and smelled the bacon starting to fry.

"Boy, mister, that sure does smell good."

"It'll be good, too. Do you drink coffee?"

"Sure do. I like it strong," he said, as he poured water into Daniel's coffee pot.

"My name is Daniel. What's yours?"

"Don't tell anyone. It's Tommy Joe Collins, but they call me TJ."

"Well TJ, what has put you out here by yourself? Where'r your parents?"

He looked at Daniel, tears flooding his eyes. "Indians killed my Pa, and taken my mother with them. They never seen me."

"When did this happen?"

"Today, about noon time."

"Do you know which way they went with your mother?"

"Yes, sir, I followed them for a while. They found the wine that Pa makes from the mustang grapes growing along the creek near the house. They took three jugs; they're probably out of their heads by now. That stuff is purdy strong."

"Can you show me where they are?"

"Shore, they's just over that hill, yonder. I seen 'em there earlier."

Daniel got up. "You stay right here and eat; I'll go take a look. How many are there?"

"Theys four or five of 'um. They got guns. They shot up the house. That's when Pa got hit."

"Well, a boy your age shouldn't be alone in this world. I'll see if we can do somethin' about your Mom."

Daniel went to his saddle and pulled his rifle from the boot the headed toward the hill on the other side of the creek. He waded across the shallow creek which had a hard rock bottom.

When he got close to the top of the hill, he started to crawl. Once he moved high enough to see over it, he saw the fire and heard the laughing. One laughed so hard he fell and rolled over.

Daniel surveyed the location and determined there were four. Off to the side was the boy's mother, tied hand and foot to a small tree.

He thought, *they will pass out before long; then I should be able to just walk in and untie the lady.* He relaxed and watched.

One mockingly offered the wine jug to the woman. Daniel pulled the hammer back on his rifle, but the Indian drew the jug back to himself and laughed. After about thirty minutes, three had passed out; the fourth was just finishing off the last jug of wine. He turned it up to drain the very last drop. The jug dropped from his hands and he rolled over, out cold.

Daniel walked down into the low place where they had made camp. The woman's eyes widened when she saw Daniel. He put his finger to his lips to insure her silence, untied her and told her which direction to go in a hurry. He stayed behind to make sure she got away before the Indians could see what direction went.

He came back with their guns, leading their four horses. "I think these horses and guns are a small recompense for what they've done to you." He could see their reunion had been a happy one.

Mrs. Collins looked up as Daniel approached. "He says your name is Daniel. I can't thank you enough for what you've done for TJ and me," she said as tears filled her eyes.

"I know how it is to be separated from your son. I'm glad I could help. "No thanks are necessary, Mrs. Collins. Things like this usually don't turn out so well. Do you have someone you can stay with? Those Indians know where you live and they may come back. They are afoot now and off the reservation; it shouldn't be long before you can move back home. I'm very sorry about your husband. I know it will be hard for a while, and you may have to make a move. I'm not sure TJ can manage your farm. I'm headed to the Indian agent's office at Muskogee; maybe he'll send someone to take care of these stray renegades."

"My sister lives west of here. Not too far, I think."

"Do you know the way?"

"I do! It's not far," spoke up TJ.

"Okay then. I'll help you on the horses."

He lifted TJ on to one horse and then helped Mrs. Collins on another. He gave each the lead ropes to take the two extra horses.

"I hope you will be comfortable on the Indian saddle, Mrs. Collins."

"The name is Velva, Daniel. Thank you again."

As they rode off, it struck Daniel that Velva wasn't very old herself, and was very nice looking. He muttered to himself, "She shouldn't have trouble finding another Pa for TJ . . . if she has a mind to."

Daniel gathered up all of his things, scrubbed out his skillet at the creek, put them in the pack, and continued on his journey.

Ten days later, he arrived at the home of the Indian agent for the Three Rivers reservation.

After tying the horses to the hitching rack, he knocked on the door. John Severs opened it and his face lit up in a wide grin. "Flo, come see who's here!"

Florence Severs presented Daniel with a big smile and threw her arms around him. "Oh' Daniel, it's been so long. Where have you been? How's Jennifer, and your boy? Come in and sit down. We've sure missed you; it's been so long." When she noticed the sad look on his face, she asked, "What is it Daniel? Has something happened?"

John Severs interrupted her. "Slow down, Flo; give him a chance to answer."

"John and Florence . . . I hate to tell you this, but Jennifer and our son, Adam, were murdered on our way to a job in North Texas."

Her face dropped and tear welled up in her eyes. "Oh no! Oh, Daniel, I'm so sorry to hear that. We've missed you and Jennifer so much," she said weeping into her apron.

"I came so that Laughing Dove could know and morn. Will you tell her for me; I'm not sure I can face her?"

"She won't blame you, Daniel, but she will want to see you," Flo explained.

"In the morning then, but I must get back home; I have a job, and there is work to do."

"John, if I can I would like to buy grain from you to get my horses ready to make that long trip home. There is not much for grazin' on in some places the way we came. We did have good grass part of the way. Where the grass does get thin, the grain will keep them goin'."

John stood. "Sure. I'll take care of your horses, Daniel; you've had a long trip. I'll see that they have plenty of grain, and I'll put some in a bag to take with you."

Florence stood. "What am I thinking? You need some food yourself. It will only take a minute; the stove still has coals, and supper is not even cold yet."

He followed her into the kitchen. "I thank you, Flo, it's has been a long time since I've had a good meal. By the way, can I still buy supplies in the store?"

"You sure can. We got in a lot of things yesterday."

When John came back in, from taking care of the horses, he told Daniel, "I sent little John to let Laughing Dove know you are here; she will come tomorrow. Meanwhile, you'll stay here with us."

"I appreciate it, John."

"You're more that welcome, Daniel, and I'm sure sorry about Jennifer. She was a wonderful girl. Do you mind telling us what happened?"

"Not at all," and he explained exactly what happened.

"I would have come earlier, but I was shot, too, and didn't even know who I was for some time. By the way, John, four renegades shot a Mister Collins and took his wife hostage about seventy or eighty miles south of here. I thought you might send someone to check. I don't know if they were yours, but they were so drunk, I relieved them of their hostage along with their horses and guns, so unless they steal horses, they are afoot."

Mr. Severs shook his head and laughed at the way Daniel told his story.

"I'll tell the reservation police tomorrow, Daniel, and thanks."

Next morning, Laughing Dove came to the house. She chanted for a minute in Cheyenne, and then threw her arms around Daniel, trying her best to not burst out crying.

After visiting with Laughing Dove and the Severs, Daniel bid them goodbye and headed back home.

Twenty-nine days later he rode up the livery. "Well, hello, Daniel. I 'bout thought you wasn't comin' back."

"I don't want to make that trip again anytime soon! Take care of the horses and put the extra on my bill. I gotta get a bath and something to eat."

"Will do, Dan'el; see you tomorrow."

Daniel walked to the boarding house, stepped up on the shaded porch, and stopped in the doorway. A cool breeze was making its way from the back door to the front. He didn't move, soaking up the coolness.

Grace saw him standing there and ran to him. "Why are you standing in the doorway?"

"I haven't been this cool in days."

"I thought you had abandoned us. You realize you were gone long enough for all of us to worry about whether you were coming back or not."

"Oh, so you missed me."

She popped him on the shoulder. "You know we did!"

"Georgia, too?" he asked.

"She just said, a while ago, I'm sure glad I don't have to keep fixing food packets for him!"

"Now, Grace, that doesn't sound like Georgia I know. Are you sure?"

She threw her arms around him and kissed him.

"I'm awfully dirty, Grace."

"I don't care. I'm just glad you're back."

"Not as much as I am. That was a long trip. Longer and harder than a trail drive! Let me bathe and shave, and I sure would like one of your steaks."

"I'll go start one. Give me a minute . . . I'll be right back."

"Okay, the steak's cooking. Tell me about the trip."

"Well, it was pretty uneventful."

"Uneventful? You had an uneventful trip? That's hard to believe!" she teased.

"Well, there was this one thing, I guess. I ran into a kid about Adam's age, crying by a big fire. When I asked him about it, he said his pa was killed by Indians and his mother had been taken prisoner." He paused.

"Don't stop there, for goodness sake! What happened?" she blurted out.

"Not much, really; they stole his pa's extra strong mustang wine, so after they passed out, I just walked into their camp, untied his mother, and sent her and TJ off to her sister's.

I told Mister Severs about the renegades and he said he would send someone to check on them. That's about it."

"Just walked in and untied her? Just like that? Sounds pretty exciting to me!"

"Yasir, and does to me too," said Georgia, who, unbeknownst to them, had been standing nearby listening to the story.

"Other than that, it was uneventful, like I said. I was just glad I was there to help."

CHAPTER 17

When Daniel walked back into the dining hall, Grace was coming out of the kitchen carrying an order. As she passed him she said, "You sure clean up nice."

"Why, thank you ma'am. What's your name? I may call on you later."

She looked over her shoulder and remarked, "You wish . . . I don't entertain strange callers."

He sat at his usual table, back to the wall to see the door. Soon, Georgia brought out his steak cooked just the way he liked it with all the trimmings and still sizzling."

He looked up and smiled. "I hear you were glad I wouldn't be asking for you to fix me food, thinking I wouldn't be coming back."

"Why, who told you that? Musta been somebody don't want me takin' care of you."

He gazed at the steak with a big smile. "Could be, but I'm sure glad it's not the case. Only way anybody could get me away from your cookin' is if it tastes like jerky, which I've been eating a lot of the last two months!"

"Well, dig in. If that aint's enough, you call me, honey. I'll take good care of you."

Grace came to his table and sat down.

"You have no idea how much we missed you."

He looked up at her with a cut of steak on his fork and a lifted eyebrow and asked. "*We*?"

"Well, you know what I mean . . . Me, I missed you. I like having you around."

"It's good to be back. I had a lot of time to think. I would like to tell you what I think, later if you have time," he said.

"I'll make time," she said as she went back into the kitchen.

Returning to Daniel's table with a coffee pot, she asked, "Just what is it you think?"

"Will it be all right to meet you in your room after a while? I'd like a kiss or two."

"Sure! Anytime you're ready."

"I can't be ready 'till I finish my steak!"

Later, as he entered her room, she met him just inside the door, threw her arms around him, and they kissed.

"Do you want to talk now or later?" she asked, still in his arms.

"I'd rather stay just like this, but we better talk, for I have so little resistance," he said smiling down at her.

"I've been thinking I should go to our house and work for a week or so to get all the outside up to date, and then we can work together on the inside. Besides, if the outside looks new when you come to work on what you want to change, you'll feel more like fixin' it up."

"That sounds about right; but we need to talk about what we are to do about the boarding house."

"We have four hundred and fifty cattle to call our own, not including the breeding stock.

At twelve dollars a head, that puts us in pretty good shape. With my job helping Brian, we can make it okay."

She mulled that over in her mind for a minute and said, "Georgia may take it on and share a little with us, too."

He smiled. "So, we have it all worked out."

"Not so fast . . . we still have to sell Georgia on this idea."

"Let me fix up the place first, and then we can ask her; unless you can figure a way to start hinting about it.

"Honey, I'm going over to the hardware store to get enough fencing from Barney to make a kind of court yard. Will white paint for that and the house be okay with you?"

"Yes, that will be nice. When do you plan to go?"

"I'll pick up a wagon load and leave in the morning. It'll take a little longer in the wagon. Anything you want me to take for you?"

"Nothing until we get it cleaned up inside. I sure wish I could go with you; you've been gone so long."

"I know. I'll see you at supper."

A quick kiss and he was out the door.

Daniel pulled the wagon up to the hardware store, jumped up on the dock and headed to the big doorway. Barney looked up over his eyeglasses at Daniel.

"Hello, Daniel. You gonna buy me out today?"

"Not today, Barney; I just need some fencing and some paint."

"So happens I got both!"

Daniel selected the straightest boards he could find for the fence and picked up several gallons of paint. "That ought to do it, Barney; at least I think it will."

"That's a bunch of boards, Daniel; you gonna take it all under fence"

"Nope, just a courtyard and a new gate. Put it on my bill, Barney; I may need more."

"Okay, Daniel. Thanks."

He tied the load on and placed the wagon in the yard of the livery. "Keep an eye on it for me, Chester."

"Sure, nuf," Chester replied.

Next morning he ate breakfast then headed to the livery.

"Mornin', Chester"

"Mornin', Dan'el"

"I see you've already got the team harnessed and ready to roll."

"I aim to please."

"I'll be gone a few days; I guess I had better take Latigo with me, so take care of my other horses. If Grace wants to ride, fix ole Sunshine up for her and put it on my bill."

"Won't have to do that. Help for Grace is free here."

"Much obliged, Chester." Daniel put his saddle in the wagon and tied Latigo behind the wagon. "Thanks again, Chester. Be seein' you."

With a wave, he pulled out of the livery and headed north to the Holton place."

As he was leaving town he though, *I don't know why I keep callin' it the Holton place. It isn't that anymore. I think it deserves a new name. I'll work on that, but I'd better consult Grace.*

As he rode along, the steady clip clop of the horses' hooves and the rhythmic rattle of the trace chains soon lulled Daniel to dozing.

He would wake and shake his head. *This isn't good. I could fall off of here and get run over by the rear wheels!*

He pulled the wagon to a stop, got down and walked around a bit. He talked to the horses and walked some more. His mind was clearing, and he began talking to himself. "It's hard to hear with all the noise the wagon makes. I have trouble hearing if a rider is approaching. I don't like how Holton managed to have men out trying to kill me after he was in jail, but if there are others, I'd never hear them coming."

And now I'm talking to myself, he thought as he checked in all directions. A prairie chicken called out and got an answer. Satisfied no one was near; he jumped back on the wagon, popped the reins, and was off again.

Arriving at the ranch, he began unloading the lumber. He had just gotten started when he looked up and saw two men riding toward the ranch. He picked up the rifle he had leaned against the end of the wagon, took the thong off his gun in the holster, and leaned against the last post he had put down.

He didn't move until they were close to the house. *Don't believe I've seen either one. Wait, I recognize the short one on the left. I saw him at the XIT.* Then he realized they both looked familiar.

"You fellers step down and rest awhile. You come from the ranch today?"

"That we did. We came to help get the place in shape."

"Dang, how'd you know I was here? What if I hadn't been?"

"We'da went to work on it anyway. The sheriff wired the boss; he told us to come and stay as long as it took."

"I can't tell you how much I appreciate it."

"Boss said you'ud put us up."

"And that I will. I may have to shoot an antelope, but we'll make it even if I have to go back to town."

They began helping him unload the rest of the lumber, and then began putting in posts.

"By the way, I'm William . . . call me Bill; and this is Thomas. Boy, that's a lot of lumber. What are you building?"

"Just got it to put a little white fence around the court yard, and maybe a gate, so's it looks pretty for the little woman."

Bill grinned widely. "Know what you're talkin' about. I was married once."

"She didn't like the cowboy life?" Daniel asked.

"Wasn't that; she just wanted a cowboy with a bunch o' money. How long you been married, Daniel?"

"Well, right now I'm not married. I was married before."

"Your lady like money better'n you, too?"

"No, the feller that lived here shot her and my son."

"He the one shot you too?"

"Yep."

"Dang, an' you gonna live here now?"

"Well, he didn't shoot us here . . . it was on the road close to Lubbock."

"I see. Well, let's get this fence built."

Before evening they had the fence and the gate finished. They stood and admired their accomplishment.

"I'm sure glad you fellers showed up. It made quick work. I couldn't a finished in a week."

"It was good the ground was soft to get the posts in as quick as we did," said Thomas.

You all go on in. You can get water easy in the kitchen to wash, but you'll have to prime the one in the back porch. You wash up and I'll be right back. If you don't mind, I'll just ride one of your horses instead of saddling mine."

"Okay, Daniel," the two of them headed to the house.

Daniel mounted one of the horses, took his rifle and rode out toward a tank that had been dug to catch water for the cattle. Last weeks' rain had topped it off and the wildlife got their water there. He tied his horse to a small mesquite and proceeded on foot, slowly approaching from behind the dam of dirt that had been pushed up. He eased up to see over the mound, and two antelope were watering. He eased his rifle up and took the shot. One fell; the other raised his head, but couldn't see Daniel. Daniel rose above the dam and when the other antelope saw him, it wandered away.

As Daniel was putting the small animal on the horse, the horse shied a bit but finally allowed him to throw the antelope over the saddle and climb aboard himself.

Back at the ranch, the animal was skinned and steaks were cut. Their supper was on the way.

"Daniel, you serve a good meal for fellers that came uninvited."

"I have to make a special effort for help like you two gave me today. I can go back home and get married quicker, maybe."

"Maybe we ain't done you no favor by speedin' up your marriage, Daniel," Bill said with a smile on his face.

"Quite the contrary, boys; and if you don't mind, I'll leave all my food and meat here with y'all and you can stay a while. I'll go back to town and come back with more food and supplies in a couple of days. Maybe y'all can start the painting and I'll help finish up when I get back. I planned to paint it all white. You fellers enjoy the scenery."

"We'll enjoy the steaks, but scenery? What's that mean? I kinda have a feelin' Tom Sawyer just put it over on us."

Daniel laughed, "I gotta get food if we are all gonna stay here and work."

He saddled up Latigo and headed back to town.

CHAPTER 18

Daniel sat down in his favorite chair in the restaurant. As soon as he did, Grace had a cup and a coffee pot ready for him.

"You're back awfully quick; run out of supplies?"

"Nope, ran out of food."

"Ran out of fo....? What? After all you took?"

He smiled. "Had two other hungry men to feed."

"Are you taking in boarders out there?" she asked as she sat down opposite him.

"Nope, Charles sent a couple of his men to help. The sheriff wired him what I was doing. I'm glad I stopped in the see Brian before I left. I'm going to get more supplies and food and go right back. Now, have you said anything to Georgia?"

Georgia was bringing the coffee pot around to top off his cup and was close enough to overhear. "What chew s'pose to say ta Georgia, anyways?"

Grace ducked her head a bit and looked the other way.

In a voice just above a whisper, Daniel said, "I guess you haven't."

He looked up at Georgia. "Sit down, Georgia, please."

"I is not a guest . . . I is a cook and waitress!"

"Well, there are no other customers to wait on right now, so have a seat; let's talk."

"What chew wanna talk about?" she asked eyeing them suspiciously.

"Just sit and I'll tell you."

"You wantin' me to fix another rode lunch box?"

"No, ma'am; we just want to talk."

She sat opposite Daniel. "Okay, let's talk, but we may have customers come in any minute now."

"We've got a situation that we hope you can help us with. Grace and I want to get married . . ."

Georgia leaned back and let out a cackle saying, "Lord-o-mercy, that's not news...and it's about time! Grace, honey, I tolls you so!"

"Yes, you did, Georgia, but that's not exactly what we want to talk about."

Georgia looked confused. "Oh?"

Daniel leaned a little closer to her and said, "We want to know if you and your sister, May, we know she likes to cook, too, would like to run the boarding house."

Her hand flew to her chest. "Cook and run da hotel, too?"

"Yep, the hotel, too! You would keep most of the money and pay the help at first, and right now we would need to depend on part of the money until we can get some income from our cattle."

Grace watched Georgia's face trying to gauge her reaction. "May is good with figures and I can show her all the books and how I've kept them. You know and love about everybody in town, so you have a head start."

After a long pause in the conversation, Daniel asked, "What do you think?"

The smile on Georgia's face grew until her eyes almost closed. "I thinks I can do it! I'm willin' to try just to see you two get married."

She let out another big laugh. "Lawsy me, if that ain't somethin'. I's a cook, a waitress, and now I's a manager!"

"We want to live on the ranch north of town when we get it fixed up, but I'll be available if you have any trouble." said Grace

She saw a customer come in and rose to wait on him, "Grace, honey, you tell me when the wedding is, 'cause I's gonna fix a weddin' supper like you never seen!"

Daniel looked at Grace. "I guess that takes care of it!"

"Yes, and I thank you for asking her. I've been dreading it . . . I don't know why."

"Seemed pretty easy, once we got into it. I have to load some food and supplies and get back to the house; Bill and Thomas will be getting hungry. I'll just get it at the store, honey. I'll see you in a few days."

He kissed her, looked into her eyes and kissed her again then left.

Daniel only spent a week and two days taking care of everything needed to improve the house with Bill and Thomas' help.

"I expect you two need to get back to work at the ranch. I thank you for all your help, and please let Charles know that I thank him for sending y'all. The place is ready for anyone who needs to work in this area. I'll stock supplies and be ready. It's time for me to get married!"

Thomas smiled at him. "Best of luck on that matter. We'll see you again soon. Glad to know we have a place to stay here."

"Bring a branding iron with you when you come. Don't need it now, but hoping to later."

Bill stepped up extending his hand. "It was a pleasure working with you, Daniel; hope to see you again soon."

Daniel watched them ride off toward headquarters then turned, took the lead ropes of Sunshine and Latigo, tied them to the wagon, and headed back to town.

He stopped at the livery and took care of Sunshine and Latigo, letting Chester handle the team. However, before going to the boarding house, he went to the sheriff's office.

As he stepped into the doorway, Brian turned from the pot bellyed stove and put the coffee back on it. "Been wonderin' when you'd get back. Did you get finished?"

"With my part, I guess. I wouldn't be if you hadn't wired Charles. He sent a couple of his boys to help me and we turned it out real quick. Decoration's not done yet, but we'll get on that as soon as Georgia takes over the place."

"Georgia takin' over the hotel and all?"

"Yep, hotel and all. Not much will change. She *is* the place anyway. Grace didn't have to do much. We are thinkin' of bringing her sister, May, in to be part of it, too.

Brian offered coffee to Daniel.

"I'm good, thanks"

"Thought I'd offer to do the night rounds with you tonight, if you like."

"That'll be fine; come back about six this evenin' and we'll tuck 'em in."

Daniel went to the hotel and cleaned up, put on a fresh shirt and pinned on his deputy badge.

At six, Daniel arrived at the sheriff's office and they started making the rounds of the town. As they walked the streets, most all the town's folks greeted them both. Daniel had become well known because of his episode of having lost his memory.

Jacob Higgindorf, owner of the mercantile, called out to Daniel "When's the day, Daniel?"

"Real soon now, Jacob, You got the groom's gift picked out yet?"

"Don't expect too much, Daniel; you owe me anyway. That 'to be' wife of yours has been buying material for her wedding dress, and for the others, too, and putting it on your bill."

"Others? What others?"

"Guess you've never attended a wedding, before, if you don't know about the *others*. They are called bride's maids.

"Guess I never thought about what goes into a wedding. Maybe I can talk her into running away."

That won't be any cheaper; I've got this no return policy for wedding clothes!" He chuckled as he turned back into his store.

"You know, Brian, I just realized I don't have any clothes fit for a weddin'."

Brian looked at him and said, "I 'spect that was what Jacob was hinting. Better go on in and pick somethin' out."

"Think that'll make him happy?"

"Likely so," he said with a chuckle.

Daniel went into the store, walked over to Jacob and said, "Okay, I'm takin' the hint. What do you have in the way of weddin' clothes that'll meet the high standards?"

"Well, you are a bit larger than Ned Birk."

"Jacob, Ned's been dead a week or two."

"I know that, Daniel, but they ordered a couple of suits to make sure they had a fit, and only took the one they buried him in."

"So . . . you're telling me you want me to buy the other suit that he could have been buried in?"

"Well, he never had it on; the other one fit, first try!"

"Well, trot it out and let's see if it fits."

Jacob brought him the suit and he stepped into the back room to try it on. When he came out, Brian and Jacob both carried on about how good he looked in it.

"It does feel like a good fit; but if either one of you says anything about this being to burry ole Ned in, you'll never hear the last of it."

He removed the suit, put on his own clothes and stepped out, telling Jacob, "I'll need a white shirt; you ought to throw one in since I'm takin' the suit off your hands. Oh, and maybe a tie!"

"I'll do that, Daniel; consider it your wedding gift for the groom."

Daniel and Brian continued to make the evening rounds.

As they walked along Brien said, "Looks to me like everyone in town knows you. You ought to make them feel safe when you are seen making the rounds. I may just let you make them from now on."

"That'll be fine, Brian."

The sheriff headed back to the office and Daniel went to supper.

As he walked into the office of the hotel, Grace came to meet him. "You stayed longer than I thought," she said walking into the restaurant with him. "I expected you back sooner. Any problems?"

"No problems. Sorry, Grace. I walked the rounds with the sheriff. I thought I needed to, since he gave me the deputy job."

"How did that go?" she asked.

"Real well, I think. Everyone was real friendly."

"Sit down and I'll bring you something."

"Good I'm starved. Georgia say anything more?"

"Nope, but she sang all day, and never stops grinnin', so I know she's happy."

Daniel looked up and Georgia was headed his way with a plate loaded with food.

"Boy, now that's service! I just got set down."

After dinner, Grace and Daniel went to her room to make plans.

"Grace, why don't we skip having a big wedding and have the preacher marry us over at his office?"

"You can't be serious! We . . . or, at least, I . . . have made plans and just about have all we need complete."

"When do you plan for it to take place?"

"Let's decide that now, together."

He could see tears forming in her eyes, so he took her in his arms. "I'm sorry, honey. I know it means a lot to you, and I'm sorry I even mentioned rushing it, but I would like it to be soon."

"As would I. I was thinking maybe next Saturday."

"NEXT Saturday? That sounds good to me. You know I'm ready," he agreed. "I bought a suit today. Don't tell anybody, but I expect a big discount."

"Why is that," she asked.

"I took it off Jacob's hands. He had ordered it for Ned Birk."

"Ned Birk? Dan, he's dead!"

"I know, but they ordered two suits to be sure one fit. Luckily, the first one fit, so this one has never been tried on, until I did today. Grace, honey, I'm ready! Now, don't you tell anyone about that suit business. I've already threatened Brian and Jacob, so don't make me threaten you, too."

She had trouble stopping her laughter. "Your secret is safe with me, but don't be surprised if word doesn't get out anyway. Jacob lets things slip occasionally."

"I suppose most of the townsfolks were invited to the wedding."

"Daniel, I just hope I haven't overlooked anyone. That would be awful! Can you think of anyone we haven't invited?"

"I don't know . . . maybe the governor."

"No, I sent him an invitation."

"You didn't really, did you?"

She laughed. "No, silly, But I thought about it! It would be nice to have someone important."

"What about me? Am I not important?"

"Oh, you know what I mean."

"I know. You were so uptight I thought I'd josh you to break the tension.

"You did send one to Charles."

"Yes, but not really expecting him to come; it's so far and he's so busy."

"He may surprise you."

Hesitantly Daniel asked, "Do you think we could have it outside?"

"As sure as we do, it will rain; besides Margarete is going to supply the music and the organ is inside the church, so does that answer your question?"

"I believe it does; let's have it inside." He smiled. "Anything else I should be taking care of?"

"You could see if Georgia needs anything else in order to prepare the food."

"Will do . . . I could use something sweet right now."

"Well, here then," she leaned over and kissed him. "There, how's that?"

"It will have to do until I can find another one on the street somewhere."

"Oh, you! Get out of here!"

He headed to the door and she gave him further instructions. "Don't go up and down the streets looking for a kiss like that, because you won't find it."

"I may look anyway; see ya."

Brian and Jacob's wives, Beth and Dora, had placed strings of laced material all around the auditorium of the church, and placed a decorative archway where the preacher and the bride and groom would stand.

Dora said, "All and all I think it looks lovely."

Beth agreed. "Not much else we can do to make it look any better!"

Grace walked up and also agreed. "You two have gone above and beyond on this place; I just don't know how I can thank you."

"You don't have to, Grace; we feel you are part of the family.

Tears welled and Grace began to cry.

"Did we say something wrong, Grace?"

"No. Not at all . . . It just makes me feel so good to be thought of as family."

Dolly spoke up. "We mean it, Grace. You are like family. You've done so much for our community. Why are you crying? Cheer up. You've fed our families when we couldn't. You provided a place to stay when the Gibson's house burned. Who in town has done more than you, Grace?"

"Thank you. I was just thinking when we move out to our house, I won't see you as often."

"Sure you will, Grace. You'll be able to spend the day with any one of us once Georgia takes over the boarding house."

Drying her tears, she responded, "I guess so. Anyway, thank you both for what you've done for us . . . for our wedding."

Beth said, "It's been our pleasure."

"Well, I think everything is about ready for tomorrow." Grace turned and asked, "You both have your dresses and everything that you need for the ceremony don't you?"

"We do, so don't worry," Beth replied.

"I'm going over to make sure Georgia has everything she needs. I'll see you two tomorrow."

They said their goodbyes and left.

Grace went to the boarding house and joined Georgia in the kitchen.

"Georgia, is there anything you need that I can get for you?"

"Yessum, I got everything, except one thing."

"And what is that, Georgia. I'll get it for you."

"I gots my Sunday clothes, but I needs that little hat Mista Jacob has on that hat rack by the material counter with the little purple flowers on it."

"I can do that right now . . . are you sure there is nothing else you need?"

"No, ma'am, that's all."

"Okay, I'll be back."

Daniel was coming back in as Grace was leaving. She said, "Daniel, stay right here. I'll be right back, we need to talk!"

"Yes ma'am ... I'm not in trouble, am I?"

"Should you be?" she replied as she continued out the door.

He laughed and wagged his head as he went to the back and sat down. "Women!"

Georgia stood in the kitchen door, smiling. Daniel looked up and asked, "What?"

"Nothing, Mista Fleming, I's just lookin'."

"And why are you smiling?" he asked.

"Cause, Miz Grace is getting' me a hat to wear to da wedding."

"Well, that's nice Georgia, and you can wear it to church too."

"Yasir, I can. It shore is purdy."

"When Grace gets back, you'll have to model it for us."

"Yasir, I will . . . I'll shore do that. Mista Daniel, you needs one of these little sweet things I done made. Kinda try it out an' let me know how it is."

"I can sure do that, but better let me have it before Grace gets back."

She brought him a sweet with a napkin.

"Thank you, Georgia." He took a bite, paused a moment, and smacked his lips. "Georgia, you better make a bunch of those; they will go fast!"

"Thank you, Mista Daniel."

"How about another one before Grace gets back?"

She brought him another.

When Grace returned with the hat, she placed the box on the counter.

"Oh! I does thank you, Grace. I done told Mista Daniel I would model it for him."

Grace smiled. "Of course! Try it on, Georgia."

She put it on and Grace adjusted it for her. "It was made for you, Georgia!"

Georgia fairly waltzed into the room to show it to Daniel. "Well, Mista Daniel?"

"What's with the Mister Daniel bit? Just call me Daniel."

"It's the hat she wants you to see, Daniel."

"Oh! I'm sorry, Georgia. That is plumb captivating."

"I don't know what that means . . . is it good or not?" she said looking at first Grace then Daniel.

Grace spoke up. "It means it looks not just good, but special good."

"You are going to steal the show at the wedding, Georgia."

"I don't wants to steal no show; I just wants Hurley Johnson from over at the blacksmith shop to see me."

"Why Georgia, we had no idea you had eyes on a certain man! He will be hooked when he sees you in that hat." They both agreed.

"Daniel, you did invite Hurley didn't you?

"Yes, I did and I told him Georgia was cookin' a big meal. He said he would be here with bells on. And speaking of a big meal, Georgia, I'd like for you to put all the left overs that won't spoil in a box for Grace and me to take with us after the wedding."

"I can do dat. I'll have it ready. Where does you plan to go?"

"Don't tell her," he said, in a whisper while pointing to Grace. "But I plan to take her to see a real landmark; have you ever heard of the Palo Duro canyon?"

Georgia drew her eyebrows together and squished her face up. "No, sir, I don't thinks I have. Is it a long way off?"

"Not really. It's this side of Amarillo."

"I've heard of Amarillo afore. So I gots a good idea where it is."

"Well, I rode through it the other day; and it's something to see, so I really want her to see it."

"I reckon she will love it, Mista D.

Saturday came, the wedding took place without a hitch and when it was over, Georgia stood and announced, "Ya'll escuse me, but I done promised a big banquet for these two an' I gots a lots of food, so you better meet over at the boardin' house right away afore the men folks eat it all up, and so as to let these two gets to what you gets to after a weddin'!"

* * * *

About the author

David Gene Dodge was born in Electra, Texas in 1930. His father, Earl Dodge, a veteran of World War I, met his mother, Pearl Kelley, as she worked in a boarding house in the oil fields, owned by her mother.

He is a graduate from Texas Tech College, now Texas Tech University, in 1951 with a BS degree in Agricultural Education. He worked his first round-up at the age of fifteen on the Triangle ranch, once a part of the Four Sixes ranch conglomerate; and filmed the round-ups on other large ranches.

Upon graduation he worked for Consolidated Vultee aircraft (Convair) building B36 bombers.

He taught electricity and electronics for aircraft in the A&E school for the Air Force at Sheppard Air Force Base, in Wichita Falls, Texas.

From there he went into Television at KFDX-TV in Wichita Falls, where he spent ten years, the start of sixty three years in television and films, working all over the United States and overseas.

He has ridden the trails, and cooked from the chuck wagon.

His love for the cowboy life has brought him, at the age of eighty eight, to writing fiction about, settling the West, his name for the series of five books that he has on Amazon.

Settling the West series tells the story of individuals who have gone into the west to make a home.

He has a love for backpacking that has taken him to the bottom of Grand Canyon a couple of times and into the Rockies and the Smoky Mountains. He admits that time has passed him by in this sport, as his "muscles don't work like they used to".